T0164649

The *Rustlers* from *Caliente Creek*

The *Rustlers* *from* *Caliente Creek*

Dick Coler

Order this book online at www.trafford.com
or email orders@trafford.com

Most Trafford titles are also available at major online book retailers.

© Copyright 2011 Dick Coler.
All rights reserved. No part of this publication may be reproduced, stored in a retrieval
system, or transmitted, in any form or by any means, electronic, mechanical, photocopying,
recording, or otherwise, without the written prior permission of the author.

Printed in the United States of America.

ISBN: 978-1-4269-7027-6 (sc)
ISBN: 978-1-4269-7028-3 (e)

Trafford rev.05/16/2011

www.trafford.com

North America & International
toll-free: 1 888 232 4444 (USA & Canada)
phone: 250 383 6864 ♦ fax: 812 355 4082

Dedicated to family and friends
. . . and all my Cowboy pals

CHAPTER ONE

THE NEW HORSE

It was well past noon and the sun was high in the sky, when he limped toward the corral gate to have a look at the wily bronc.

Two days seemed like a lifetime with his bad ankle hurting with each step he took, all because of that 'snaky' horse he called "Lawyer". He called him Lawyer because it was always looking for a way to get him off.

Hank's ankle was twenty years older than the four year old gelding who was eying him from behind the cedar corral poles. Hank was hobblin' all right, but he had wrapped his foot pretty tight so he could squeeze it into his left boot. He guessed it wasn't broken and after all, the swelling had gone down some.

"This bay's near 'bout broke to ride," Stubby said, last week when he brought over six 'usin' horses. Hank bought horses from Stubby before, and he was very reliable for furnishing good horseflesh. They all just weren't quite 'finished broke'.

Hank's dad and his dad's brother started this Circle Diamond ranch years ago, and both families decided to stay-it-out over the years.

Hank's mother and daddy both passed away within two months of each other two years ago. About the same time, he had gone off and got hitched-up 'double to the wagon' and brought

Abbey and about nine hundred dollars back with him from a Virginia City casino. Eight weeks later his momma died and six weeks after that he lost his dad.

Aunt Lucille and his uncle, Clyde, were holding claim on the ranch now, with nothing but goodness for Abbey and him.

Hank's two cousins, Clifton and Getwood, were a little older than he, and Clifton's wife, Caroline, was going to have her baby any day.

* * *

Lawyer was calm and quiet when Hank opened the corral gate and approached him with a few kind words. His mind was made up to use this horse this very day to look for a young bull Getwood couldn't find last week.

Hank planned to make a big circle past the Caliénte creek and close to the Blue Sand mountains, where he'd once noticed some heifers grazing. That's the place where he was heading a couple of days ago when the 'Lawyer got him off'.

"Whoa, boy," he chortled to him. "Give me time to get my sore foot in this stirrup, and I'll take you for a nice ride in this sunny, Nevada wild country."

Hank got to thinking, as he rode through the corral gate and into the sun and sagebrush, that this bay horse must have decided that by staying saddled in the corral, with his tail tied to the slicker that was hanging down from the saddle horn on one side, was a good lesson in behavior. The horse was as quiet as a trade rat.

Lawyer was responding well to the rein as they jogged over the cactus and sage that grew in profusion on the range. Lawyer was a well-muscled, good-sized horse, standing over six- teen hands tall and weighing over 1,200 pounds.

This horse grew nicely to maturity and was also above average in most every way.

"Well, boy, it's time for a faster gait if we expect to cover the base of the Blue Sands, yet today. Let's see what you got," he said, as he adjusted his seat to relieve some weight on his left stirrup.

Hank spurred him in the flanks and Lawyer bolted from the sting at a jolt that felt to Hank as though he'd fired his shotgun without holding the stock close enough to his shoulder. The horse was flat-out running and covering plenty of ground.

After a good run Hank pulled the long hackamore rein in tighter to slow down to a dog-trot jog. No sense in 'wind-breaking' a good horse just to try him out, on a warmer than usual, early fall day.

The horse didn't offer to buck any more with Hank since two days ago when he spooked-out from under him, and got his head between his front legs. They were getting more comfortable with each other. Hank knew that each time you ride a horse you're either training him or un-training him. He was hoping this was a good training session.

There he was. That young, Durham bull they'd searched after for a week or so. As Hank had expected, he was protecting six, two-year-old heifers, and they were about two hundred yards from a bend in the stream that offered sweet water from the mountains.

He decided to hold back a little and let them drink, for it was soon time to head this gather back to the home pastures, four sections away. Hank would have time, but he mustn't waste it.

He figured he'd wait another ten or fifteen minutes and then start on his way.

Hank stepped off his horse, who was ganted-up and a mite leg-weary, but not much the worse for wear. After all, he was bred to use, and Hank was using him.

They watered at a spring that was feeding into the creek and affording it some mighty cold water. He'd been in the saddle a couple of hours and when he stepped down from being horseback, his ankle was starting to ache, causing him to swear at that beautiful, big, bay horse. He knelt down to garner a share of that sweet water, and after a fill, climbed back on Lawyer, sore foot and all.

Time to start this gather on their way. The heifers were agreeable to being moved, since they had their bellies filled with cool water, and had been grazing most of the day.

The Durham bull, however, resented being urged to move from a 'garden of eden' with good graze and plenty of water, and when all the heifers started to line out, he must have figured the cowboy was spoiling his style.

Lawyer was raised up among cattle on a ranch and was familiar with their ways. He had a good amount of 'cow-sense' in him, but there was doubts if he'd ever crossed wits with a big, stout bull, before. Those little heifers started along down the trail, and when the bull was challenged to move, he worked himself into a tantrum and began to stomp and snort, and defy any interference.

Hank snaked out his rope as quick as he could, then thought better than to dab a big loop on him with no help to get another rope on him. He didn't have his dog along with him, either.

The first charge the bull made was at the horse's flank, and he hit him hard enough that Hank's sore foot came loose from his stirrup.

When the horse tried to jump out of the way, Hank lost his balance and flopped out of that saddle and onto the ground, and of course, landed smack-dab on his sore ankle. He was positive this young range bull would immediately charge him, and stomp him to pieces. Hank's thoughts flashed to Abbey and a reunion he feared wouldn't arrive.

But the bull didn't see him on the ground, he was too busy charging after Lawyer. Hank quickly dragged himself past the spring and found several big boulders. He watched the bull chase his big horse, who led him toward the the trail and the six heifers.

By now, Hank was hurting and a-foot, and feeling kind of sorry for himself. He started to grin, as he spoke aloud while thinking to himself.

"Wal, I ain't never seen a wild critter, or any other animal, fer that matter, a-feelin' sorry for itself.

CHAPTER TWO

AN IMPORTANT DISCOVERY

It looked as though it was going to be a mighty long walk for Hank to get back to Abbey and the ranch. Lawyer had run away from the red bull, but at least he was heading in the direction of the Circle Diamond ranch.

After about twenty steps, and ten yards down the trail, Hank knew he was not about to walk back to the ranch. By now, his ankle was starting to swell, and he was sure it wouldn't take him another twenty steps. He sat down near a good sized cedar tree to ponder his fate.

It wasn't but ten minutes later that he spied his new horse, that crazy bay he named the Lawyer, walking slowly back up the trail toward his cedar tree.

"Easy, son," he said, as he whistled softly at the bay. "Just take it easy, and keep on a- comin', just the way you are."

Hank whistled a low, steady type, nothing shrill, and his horse looked around to follow the sound. Cautiously, but surely, he walked up to the cowboy. Hank just as slowly reached out and scratched his neck and shoulder, while, with a low monotone, kept repeating, "Easy boy, take it easy."

He carefully cradled the reins and painfully climbed aboard. Most cowboys mount from the near side, and since he placed his sore left ankle in the stirrup, while he pulled his upper body weight with his hands on the saddle horn, winced at the sharp pain.

Had this been a finished-broke and a 'usin'-type' ranch horse, Hank would have climbed on the right side. Not with Lawyer. No sense in getting bucked off. The sun had started to bed down as Hank pushed the small gather of heifers into the corral near one of the barns. Clifton and Uncle Clyde had seen the group coming, and were at the corral to open the gate, and afford some of the hazing to get the bunch inside.

Abbey was at the gate corner to greet him and help him down from his horse. "Clifton," Clyde said to his eldest son, "take that pony and unsaddle him, while I get some feed to these cattle. Be careful, and put him in the barn with the jingle horse."

By the time Abbey helped Hank to the comfortable log cabin where they stayed, beside the main house, the moon was starting to show behind the gray clouds that gathered earlier.

"That's the gol-durnest bay horse I ever seen", Hank explained to Abbey. "He kept that ol' bull off'n me as sure as a rodeo clown would do for a bull rider, and made it chase him 'stead of me. After he led him off down the trail toward the young heifers, would you believe he came back and was lookin' for me?"

Abbey had already carefully pulled Hank's boots off and was slowly removing his britches and socks, as she prudently unwrapped her husband's tender ankle. Next, she prepared a basin with cold well water from the kitchen sink-pump, and some big towels to try to soothe the aching she knew occurred.

Hank's casual indifference suddenly became a total reversal as Abbey's gentle touches and complete sensual approach to his taut body set off a lantern light burning in his loins.

"You haven't had anything to eat since morning, sweetheart, aren't you just starved?"

"I've eaten since we've made love, you know?" he enticed a sly question.

"Don't you think Clyde and Lucille will be coming over to find out about your adventure today?"

"Just bolt the door and turn down the lamp, and slide over here beside me," he replied, as he sat upright to unfasten her blouse. "There's no cause to concern yourself over the folks. Their questions will easily wait 'til morning."

"Well, what about your supper?" her ultra-sexy voice inquired.

"It'll wait, c'mere." He finished disrobing her beautiful, show-girl body. Abbey fumbled with a button on Hank's shirt before she excitedly tore it from his broad, straight shoulders. They em-braced and were totally unclothed when the thought of Hank's injured ankle was cause for her concern, and she asked, "Hank, what about the pain?"

"You'll just have to endure it love, I will."

The swollen ankle dilemma was of not much concern for Hank the next morning. He had awakened with a ravenous approach for a true ranch breakfast. Abbey obliged his new hunger lust when she prepared eggs and beef and flap-jacks, to be washed down with real, old-fashioned, cowboy-coffee. She boiled the water and added several handfuls of fresh ground Arbuckle coffee. Hank smiled, again.

"I wish I could use my ankle for an excuse for a little while longer," Hank said, as he embraced Abbey for the hundredth time.

"You're going to saddle Lawyer this morning, aren't you?" Her red-rose lower lip was in the form of a pout, as she questioned Hank. "I guess your foot is better, the way you were carrying on last night." Hank smiled as he playfully patted her on her derriere, wrapped with a freshly-washed flour sack covering her sky-blue, denim jeans.

"You bet I am," came the answer. "He needs the work and I want Uncle Clyde to see what a powerful and usable horse that he's turning out to be."

The morning sun was playing tag with the blue-gray clouds as Hank made his way to the horse barn that morning. He'd said his sad so longs to Abbey inside their tastefully decorated cabin. He told her to find Getwood and have him harness the sorrel team, so she could drive into Walker Lake, today.

"Aunt Lucy wants me to go with her over to Hawthorne. It's only a little bit farther, We need to get the larder filled."

"Fine with me," he said, over his shoulder. "I guess I'll see you at supper." The moment he spoke he could see the reaction of his ardent wife as she held her arms askew, while her body silently motioned for his acceptance. Hank reluctantly forced himself toward the barn, knowing the ranch work came first.

Abbey waved, as she held her thoughts in check. Oh, how she ached to hold him once more before he rode out of the ranch.

Lawyer nickered softly as Hank approached the barn and had his first morning inspection of the big bay. "You're really a good-lookin' horse," he remarked. "I'll toss you some grain to go with that alfalfa, and I'll get some for ol' Brownie, too."

The jingle horse was just about as glad to see Hank as Lawyer was. All his hay was gone, also. Hank forked some to both horses as Getwood appeared in the doorway.

"Listen, Hank, I'm 'bout fed-up with takin' orders from you or that doe-eyed ol' whore you're a-humpin'. Daddy's still ramrod on this outfit, and . . ." SPLAT! Getwood's eyes rolled back in his head, and the blood spilled out from the corner of his mouth, as he desperately tried to stand. Hank picked him up and was ready to thump him again, as Getwood's torso slid to the straw-covered, stable floor. Hank wanted to wait for Get to regain consciousness, but decided to leave him and go.

* * *

Ol' Brownie was dead when Clyde walked in the barn after breakfast. The gelding had his throat cut. Getwood was staggering about the stall area with his Barlow knife still in his hand, when Clyde spoke.

"What in the name of God, have you done to that horse?"

"Wal, Pap, I come to git some harness for the team, and when I passed by that spooky gelding, he just kicked me in the head, for no reason at all."

"You empty-minded . . . idiot. There's absolutely no call for a reaction the likes of what you did. You have been causing us trouble on this ranch since the early days of your dismal life." Clyde was thoroughly disgusted.

Hank's dad had given him reasons as to why Getwood had served prison time. He was convicted of second-degree murder when a stage coach was held up by a gang of which he was a part. The driver was killed and the helper was critically wounded. Aunt Lucy was a cousin of the slain driver and she felt she could help ease family pain by forgiving Getwood with her liberal thoughts and offered to take him back to live and work at the Circle Diamond ranch.

"I'll never know what Lucy and I were thinkin' when we adopted you from that miserable, travelin' preacher-man. For us to take you back after the twelve years you served at Carson City, is proving to be our biggest mistake," said Clyde, upset and sad.

"Well, I'm truly sorry for whut I done, Pap. This ain't gonna happen no more, honest."

"I know that Brownie was gettin' a little old, but I never did figure he would just kick out at a person like he did, He's just never caused us any problems, and was such a good ol' horse to jingle with, he just seemed to always enjoy bein' ridden out after the cavvy, each morning," Clyde said, as he viewed the mess in the barn.

"I'll get that sorrel team hitched, Pap, and drag him off and bury him in a ditch. And no one, 'ceptin you'n me will know what a nasty ol' horse he turned out to be."

THE WEATHER IS CHANGING

Lawyer was feeling good as Hank loped him toward the East Walker river that crossed their land near the Wassuk Range of mountains, south of Walker Lake, in Mineral county, Nevada. The morning was starting to develop into some chilly temperature as the pair loped on through the range land that Hank truly loved.

He wasn't sure what he thought about Getwood, and just exactly what he was going to do about this wretched and lamentable ex-con, that Aunt Lucy so devotedly comforted, and who daily took advantage of her love.

Hank was used to remarks about Abbey. She was so beautiful and alluring that she was often seen as competition from the young women in the county, and from the matrons, too, because of her past as a saloon dancer. He chuckled to himself as he slowed down his pony and collected his thoughts.

Hank wasn't at all interested in what anyone else thought about Abbey, he knew her true worth and devotion to life and to him.

Abbey learned to cook and keep house at an early age, in spite of her chosen profession that kept her busy at night, as she grew into adult womanhood. Besides, Aunt Lucy was crazy about her, and she, Lucille.

A bond of real trust had formed. Hank was certain this was a great hurdle to overcome, that more than one woman in any household could easily get along with one another. Caroline and Abbey got along as well together as old fashioned , ranch-reared sisters.

Clifton Hall was a hard working, top hand, Nevada cowboy. Clyde taught his son very well. His Protestant work ethic was inherited from his dad, and his sense of humor and graciousness came from his mother. A fine, western ranching family, Hank decided. "How did they ever choose that bastard they call Getwood?" he said to himself, aloud.

Hank remembered asking his father years ago, when Getwood was incarcerated, why they named him that. His dad said, "His real name is Franklin Boyle, and all that preacher ever said to him was, "get wood!" He just grew up thinkin' his name really was Getwood!"

* * *

There were at least two, and maybe three, that Hank saw as he watched the ears of his pony stand up straight. He felt the horse's muscles bunch under him, and he knew, immediately, there was something nearby. This time he saw them much clearer, as he approached the fence along the south-east section near the river.

He thought they were Shoshone, or Piaute, but when he caught a glimpse of two tied horses, he saw the stock saddles, and scabbards with rifles, and he knew better. Where was the third person, Hank wondered? At last he saw him, mounted on a red-roan cow-pony, and riding along the coulee.

There were enough rocks and piñon trees to offer Hank some temporary cover. He dismounted and and silently circled the out-cropping, where he tied his horse.

Now he could see what the man who was riding the roan cow-pony was doing. He was herding a short-yearling steer along the fence line toward the other two men.

One man had a small fire going, while the other had uncoiled his rope. The fence was cut and it was no problem for Hank to figure exactly what these range rustlers had in mind.

Hank retraced his steps back to where Lawyer was tied, and cautiously lifted his Sharps carbine from it's saddle scabbard.

Hank crawled back to the scene, as Lawyer nickered - much too loud! The man at the fire pit jumped up and drew his sidearm, while his partner raced for their horses.

Hank stood up and slammed a shot at the man by the fire and knocked him down. The man who went for the horses raced in and so did the steer herder. They both dismounted and helped the wounded man onto his horse.

Meanwhile, Hank caught his bay and rode down the embankment toward the three, trying to fire his carbine at the same time. The Lawyer stumbled in his haste and rolled as he fell. Hank was tossed clear but his hopes to catch those boys were finished.

His pony jumped up, quick as Hank did, and stood there looking at the cowboy with as much as to say, "I'm not used to having a rifle fired between my ears, old friend."

They both snorted, and Hank remounted and started after the steer that by now, was through the gap in the fence. He would surely recognized that roan pony if he ever saw it again.

CHAPTER THREE

A BAD DEED - NOT YET EXPLAINED

After Hank choused the yearling steer back to his own range, and well on its way to a scattering of cattle less than a mile away, he began to mend the fence. The new horse was doing great as far as Hank was concerned, but he felt that he'd try snapping off a few more cartridges and watch the horse's reaction.

"Remarkable," Hank said aloud. The horse jumped sideways and snorted a little with the firing of the first two rounds, but then he ignored the balance of the seven rounds fired.

"You'll be ready the next time, partner," Hank told his bay horse, with some assurance that he would eagerly welcome an opportunity with those rustlers. On the way to the Circle Diamond, Hank couldn't help thinking about Getwood. Wondering what kind of a story had been told to anyone, especially how Getwood would explain his rowdy appearance to Aunt Lucy. He chuckled to himself, again.

As Hank pulled rein at the barn that late afternoon, he noticed the team and the wagon were not yet back, and he figured Abbey and Aunt Lucy were on their way home. He knew Caroline wasn't feeling well enough to arrange supper for Clifton, let alone for anyone else.

Clyde met Hank at the barn where he was busy rubbing down the coat for Lawyer and fixing to put him in the corral until tomorrow.

"Uncle Clyde, you look like someone licked all the red off your candy."

"Well, it's like this. You see, Getwood went and killed ol' Brownie early this mornin'. Must'a been 'bout the time you lit out with your new horse, 'cause I . . .'"

"What're you sayin', 'bout Getwood? That he killed ol' Brownie! Gentle ol' Brownie? what t'hell for?" Hank felt the short hairs on the back of his neck start to bristle, as Clyde started to answer him.

"Wait, wait," his uncle replied. "Getwood claimed that while he was looking for the team harness in the barn and passed by the jingle horse, that the horse retched up an' kicked Getwood in the head, jes' fer no reason at all."

"If Brownie'd kicked him anywhere but in the head, it might have hurt him," said Hank,"but the fact is, Uncle Clyde, you shouldn't believe a word he's told you. He's lyin', and I'll tell you why. Getwood and I had sort of an argument this morning, and he let his mouth run off too strong, a-sayin' things he never should've said, and I knocked him down for it."

"So," answered Clyde, "that's whut all them marks on his face is all about, his nose all swolled-up and blue and black. I'll be danged . . . an him a-layin' the blame on pore ol' Brownie, and him a-cuttin' his throat to cover his embarrassment.

He told me he was sorry for it, but - damn, boy, I'm jes not sure how Lucy's gonna take all this, her mother'n him like a baby chick and all.

She tends to look past some things that most hard folks get into and even though I'll love her forever, I'll never understand her bleedin' heart, sometimes."

"I don't suppose it's any of my business, Hank, but just whut was it that Getwood said that made you cross as bit-up bear in fly time?"

"Let it go, Uncle Clyde, maybe someday I'll tell you about it. Right now, we need to discuss something else, about what happened on our south-east range, yesterday."

The two men were starting to get deep in their conversation when Hank looked up to see the sorrel team approaching with Abbey and Aunt Lucy in the wagon.

Suddenly, out of nowhere, Getwood appeared from around the corner of the barn in time to grab the nigh horse of the team and hold them as the ladies attempted to step down from the wagon.

"Oh, Getwood, honey," Aunt Lucy exclaimed, "I am so glad to see you up and around. Abbey told me what a horrible experience you had with our jingle horse. I suppose some horses just go bad all of a sudden, but it's oh, just so terrible that he kicked you. Are you sure you're able to handle the team" I could call Clifton, or, here's Daddy and Hank. They could do it for you."

"No, momma, I'm fine. I'm a quick healer, and I did what had to be done to that crazy jingle horse. He won't be hurtin' any of us anymore. Whoa, now," he said, as he turned his direction to the sorrel team.

Abbey caught the seemlier grin on the face of Hank as he neared and howdy'd both ladies, while he extended his strong arms around Abbey's svelte waist and literally hoisted her from out the wagon. "We had a busy and exciting day, darlin', and we both have restored our souls shopping in town."

Clyde was interested in all the wrapped boxes just behind the wagon seat, while he reached for one. "Do you ladies always have to buy dry goods and foo-foo items each time you go into Hawthorne?"

Aunt Lucy just laughed at his naivete while accepting his helping hand from the wagon seat.

"You've something to tell me," whispered Abbey to Hank, as she squeezed his hand while accepting his help with some boxes. On her way to their cabin she said, "That wolfish, little-boy grin of yours does you in."

"I'll be in in a minute, love, as soon as the grain sacks are stored." He looked longingly back at Abbey.

Getwood never once looked at Hank during the entire conversations that took place at the wagon. He carefully unhitched the team and started to the barn with them intending to rub them down and feed them, and hang the harness for its next use.

All of this he did before anyone could suggest that he do this chore. Getwood finally looked back over his shoulder to see if Hank was watching him.

* * *

Wednesday morning was greeted by yet another of the famous sunrises the West continues to produce. Abbey awoke before her husband and carefully slipped away from their bed to start their morning coffee.

Abbey was certain her husband was withholding the real reason he fought with Getwood. He'd told her it was just a misunderstanding about the harness for the team, and it became heated when each lost his temper.

"I don't remember ever seein' that 'lacy-thing' you're wearin', " Hank spoke, as he swung himself from the bed and searched for his boots.

"G'mornin', sweetheart. It's just about time you shook your lazy self awake and started the day."

Hank sidled over to where Abbey was standing and talking and scooped her bronze body up in his arms.

"I'm awake, all right, and this is really the only way to start the day," he said, as he removed the 'lacy-thing' and eased her into a supine position on their bed.

Abbey quickly responded by pressing her warm, moist lips openly against his mouth and emitting a lasting, wet embrace against him.

The shutters admitted the first light from the sunrise in the eastern sky, as again, Abbey responded with taking her breath in short, quick gasps.

The tall cowboy was making slow and deliberate love with her and she was feeling his amorous motions with each heartbeat,

""You're mighty good to me," Abbey said, as she fondled the nape of his neck, while she deeply and passionately kissed his warm and stubbled face.

"You're the one that's been good for me. You've taught me so many ways of placing things in their proper perspectives, and you help me grow-up a little," Hank acknowledged.

Abbey teased Hank about crawling from their bed to light the fire in the corner fireplace.

Somehow, the early fall weather slipped up on everyone. Hank didn't bother to climb back in the bed, much to Abbey's chagrin. Instead, he stomped on his boots and then reached over and patted her on her derriere, saying, "Now who's lazy about getting up to start the day?"

The strong cowboy-coffee washed down the speckled, hen eggs and freshly-baked bread, with the mesquite-honey topping that Aunt Lucy had made just for them.

CHAPTER FOUR

DESTINY RIDES IN ON A COLD WIND

The sunrise that greeted the frosty day was bright enough for Hank to immediately notice the two riders leaving the ranch behind the barns and riding directly east, straight into a brighter than usual morning.

"Now, what d'ya think they're a-doin' this time of the day?" Hank thought to himself and said aloud. "And what kind of trouble is due?"

On his way to the barn, Clifton caught up with Hank, and together they ran into Getwood hurrying past the back side of the horse barn. Hank figured Clifton hadn't spied the two riders, but there was no mistaking the red-roan horse being ridden by one.

"Never saw you leave the house this morning, Getwood," said Clifton, as he crossed in front of his hustling step-brother. "You must've lit out before you ate."

"Yeah, howdy . . .No, er, I uh, et earlier." Get stammered with his answer. "Cliff, how's Caroline doin'?" He attempted to divert an upcoming subject.

"Dunno. I guessed today or tomorrow, uh, the weekend for certain. Seems as . . ."

"Who were you talkin' with earlier, Get?" Hank solicited an answer by directly stepping in front of Getwood.

"None of yore damn business. Some fellers I knew from some dealings in Walker Lake."

"Well, Get, did they have anything to do with those card games you were involved with last month? You promised Daddy you'd quit that habit," Clifton said, as he pulled his scarf from his neck closer to his ears.

Hank never let on to Getwood that he recognized the roan pony one of the men was riding. He would like to have another 'go' at Getwood, except that he felt it better not to involve Clifton at this time. He did figure that he'd find Getwood alone soon, and then he would have some answers.

"Well," said Clifton,"I'd better get to work on fixin' that hay rake wheel, we've got that west half-section to wind-row before any storms set in."

"I'll help you, Cliff," Getwood said, leaving Hank to go about his business with his horse. Abbey gathered all the bed linen and towels and all the other items that needed washing, including the dirty clothes, and placed them in a large basket on the front porch of their spacious log cabin.

Finished with this, she went across the yard to the main house and started to gather up all their goods that needed washing, also.

"I have the water boiling for the tubs, Abbey, dear," Aunt Lucy said, as she met Abbey in the hallway carrying one basket and sliding another with her foot.

They passed through the kitchen where Caroline was painfully trying to seat herself at the table and attempting to feed herself some rice and dry bread.

"You should be drinking milk, dear," Lucy spoke rather sternly to Caroline. Abbey set her basket aside and sat in a chair next to Caroline. With her arm on Caroline's shoulder, she desperately tried to comfort her when she wiped a tiny tear from her eye.

"It must be very hard for you to go through this process of expecting your baby, but you have to know, dear, Aunt Lucy and I are going to see to it that you're as comfortable as can be. Clifton's not going with the wagon crew on this fall's rodeer, and he can get to Hawthorne for Doc' Simmons on a very short notice."

"Abbey's right, honey," Lucille was a bit red faced that she'd spoken harshly to Caroline, well remembering the early time on the prairie when she had to deliver without the help of any trained person, and let alone, the services of a frontier doctor.

"I just know this baby's coming tomorrow," Caroline sighed. "I'm certain it's coming with some bad weather, too. It's going to be a boy, that's for sure."

Abbey offered to "redd-up" in the kitchen, but Lucy said she should go ahead and start the washing, especially since some low clouds were forming in the Nevada skies.

"Never mind the kitchen, Abbey," Lucy remarked. "Let's get you off your feet now, Caroline, and I'll tell Clifton about tomorrow and how you're feeling."

As Abbey commenced the washing, she caught a glimpse of Getwood, near the gate and decided to ask him for some help.

"Hello, Getwood," she smiled. "Could you chop some more wood for us so we can keep this fire hot under these wash tubs?"

Getwood refused to answer and was about to turn away when his mother stepped through the door to the porch. "Hi, Momma." His seedy smile was hooded by the tone in his voice. "Can I help you ladies this morning by cutting some more wood for your fires?"

"You're a sweetheart, son. Thank you so much for offering. I know you have so many chores to do, it's such a sweet thing for you to offer." Abbey was almost dumbfounded as she stood with her hands on her hips and her fists drawn tightly together, while Aunt Lucy spoke to Getwood.

Clifton was finished repairing the rake wheel, and was tending to some other business at the tool shed when Clyde approached with the women-folk news.

"You won't have no trouble a-herdin' Doc from town, will you son?"

"Last time I talked to him was ten days ago, when I took Caroline to Hawthorne for her check-up. He said he wasn't goin' hunting until next month, so he figured to be available for Caroline and for Fern Carter, 'cause she's due 'bout the same time. I seen Harry in town with Fern then. Reckon they had a 'pointment with Doc Simmons, too. Harry told me that he lost five yearlings to what he guessed was rustlers, just last month."

It was plain that Clifton was very concerned about Harry's steer loss when he answered.

"Damn, that's the third time I've heard about cattle bein' rustled here. Town folks have no idea how much it hurts ranches when they lose one little, sick calf, let alone when they lose cows to rustlers that are too corrupt to raise cattle themselves." Cliff was growing angrier with each thought. "I'll tell you, Dad, we're gonna catch those varmits soon, just wait - when we do . . ."

The sun was reluctantly shining as it nearly tendered its resignation, due to the dark cloud cover overhead.

Hank topped the ridge and rested his pony as he eased back in the saddle and then started to roll a smoke. He chose this high trail because he could look over most of their ranch. From where he sat on his horse, Hank was able to see the road and the trail that led from the back of the barn where he'd spotted the riders earlier.

* * *

The wind was fiercely fighting for its life. The eerie calls it made as it skipped among the little piñon trees, caused a weird, haunting sound. The temperature dropped considerably as the rain began. Hank crushed his smoke on the saddle leather, and hustled his horse down the embankment to the road that led the way back home.

Those gray-black clouds had boiled-up in the east, and lightning was popping all around. Hank was hammered with hail as the sun totally lost itself, and the mid-morning chill accompanied hail with sleet.

It had been a dry spell with lots of dry tanks on the ranch, so in a way, Hank was very happy with all the wet weather coming in.

"This'll likely bring us an early snowfall," Hank said to no one but Lawyer, as the horse was attempting to gain better footing on this high, malapai-rock rim. Several minutes elapsed while Hank became drenched.

* * *

WITH A WELCOME ARRIVAL-COMES BAD NEWS

Between the lightning flashes, Hank spotted the dapple-gray mare ably ridden by Getwood. This was the jingle horse that replaced Brownie.

That horse and rider were on a fast run toward the cow ranch, and Hank decided to catch up. Lawyer jumped out to a long-stride run, with Hank standing high in the stirrups, the rain and sleet pelting both.

Getwood was a hundred yards ahead and the gray was not tiring. No reason to shout, Hank knew he was seen. They'd talk when they reached home.

Clyde saw them riding in and hurried out to the barn to meet Getwood and Hank. The two were at the opposite ends of the barn, and attempting to wipe dry as much of their ponies as they could, neglecting themselves until the horses were cared for.

Hank desperately wanted to talk with Get before anything else would interfere, but Clyde was shouting to both men to hurry inside.

"S'matter, Pap?" Getwood asked.

"Hold on, Uncle Clyde," Hank interjected, as the old cow rancher sat down on a bench to catch his breath.

"We got big problems with Caroline and the baby. " Clyde's words were frenzied. "She's a-headin' down a mighty dark path. Abbey and Ma are a-doin' ever'thin' they can, but it don't . . ."

"Where's Clifton?" Hank asked him.

"He's went to fetch Doc Simmons, and he took the sorrel team. Been gone 'bout two hours, I reckon," Clyde said, visibly shaken.

* * *

The relentless, cold rain with the occasional sheets of sleet, driven by the wind, kept pouring it's slobbering wrath on the Circle Diamond cow ranch.

The baby could be heard squalling over the claps of thunder, as the men came inside the frame ranch house with it's roof of tin. The roof rattled and it shook with each gallon of water that spilled down.

"It's a boy, Hank!" Abbey joyfully said when she took the baby from Aunt Lucy. Hank was the first man to enter the bedroom and held back his breath when he saw Caroline.

She was writhing with pain and distress as Lucille was trying her best to deliver the after-birth. She was not able to comfort Caroline, who was thrashing and sobbing, trying to hold back her emotions.

Clifton and Caroline were so happy in their nine year marriage, and finally, together, eagerly anticipating their first child.

As an only child, Caroline had been coddled and adored by her father who was killed when he drove a team of mules across the railroad station tracks in Cheyenne. He came to meet her when she arrived from her eastern boarding school. She was waiting on the station platform and witnessed the fatal accident.

She met Cliff when he came out to Wyoming with the rodeo and answered the advertisement for someone to break a team of horses, at their family estate.

Caroline never quite got over the loss of her father, and became totally dependent on Clifton, as well as others, for her well being.

"We need more laudanum. Lord have mercy, she's hemorrhaging, and she's already lost too much blood." Aunt Lucy cried out, still attempting to help.

Hank took a strong hold on both of Caroline's arms, as he softly spoke while trying to comfort and quiet her.

Getwood and Clyde remained in the parlor next to the bedroom, and were contemplating what had to be done next when Abbey stepped out of the way with the tiny child still swathed and comforted in her arms.

Everyone knew better than to ask where Clifton and Doc Simmons were. With the terrible storm that befell all, it was certain that they would be very late. It appeared now, that they would be too late.

* * *

Clifton was shouting at the red team and driving for all he was worth, slapping both horses with the buggy whip, and feeding the reins as only he knew how. This was a strong team, both horses in their prime, but Doc Simmons was pleading with Clifton to slow up and save the horseflesh for fear he would drive them to their death, and they would never reach the cow ranch.

The wind in their teeth, and both the team and the passengers were agonizing with the relentless and miserable weather.

In spite of the cold and sleet, the horses profusely lathered when Clifton pulled into the ranch and leapt from the wagon, leaving Doc Simmons to himself.

Clifton raced past the front gate and up the porch steps, and burst inside as his dad was coming out to handle and care for the team.

"Getwood, find some rubbing towels and two blankets for this team. We've got to get this wet harness off and cover these horses, now hurry up."

"Caroline, honey," Clifton shouted excitedly at the doorway to their bedroom. "Oh, sweet-heart, are you . . . are you all right? Oh, Car . ."

"I'm sorry, Cliff," Hank spoke, as he met his cousin in the doorway. "Abbey and your mom done all they knew to do. The baby seems fine, but I'm truly sorry, Cliff, no one could save our sweet Caroline."

By this time the doctor was at her bedside and after a dismal moment, turned to Clifton and his mom, with a sad statement confirming that it was all over.

Clayton Cody Hall, a very healthy eight pound little boy, was in loving care hourly from 'Grandma' and Abbey. They attended the boy as if each had birthed him, and weighted him on the milk-room scale.

Clifton was nearly devastated by the turn of events, and decided to join the cowboys with the wagons. The fall round-up was delayed for several days due to the funeral, and not much work was done around the ranch.

Cliff decided his going back with the wagon crew would reduce his self-pity and accomplish a mode of ethic accountability, especially among all the cowhands.

Hank kept busy with the horses that Stubby sold him and it was a continual chore. He never once neglected his horse, Lawyer, and rode him every chance he had. Breaking young horses required a great deal of time and patience, and Hank was the kind of puncher that took his work very serious. Most did, or they would not have chosen to make cowboy'n their lifes work.

A week later saw the rodeer and branding completed. The heavy rains that blew in with the cold weather, moved east before Caroline's funeral and it enabled the family to rest her soul on a cloudless day.

CHAPTER FIVE

THE BEST LAID PLANS

The barkeep brought the whole quart of rye whisky to the table with four, big glasses, then returned to his ongoing chore of wiping off the mahogany.

It was chilly in the saloon and the pot-bellied stove was as red as a cowboy's new bandanna. Several of the local miners on the front shift were spending all their dust on beer and booze, and eyeballing the two gals doing their best to comfort the men at the Faro table.

There was a poker game ongoing near the back door. Saturday evening brought out the bar flies and the thirsty cowboys looking for ways to vent their passions, any way possible.

At the table where the whisky and four glasses were put, an interesting conversation was being discussed.

"We got twenty-nine damn good beeves all brand-changed and hidden over in Miller Canyon." Ren said, "and all's we need is a dozen more, or so, to git us a full load."

"'At damn cousin of yers near 'bout kilt me t'other week. Hadn't been fer his hoss fallin', he might would'a caught us."

"Shut up, Farris, he ain't got no idee who any of us is, an' he ain't 'bout to find out. I'll see to it. Jes you see 'bout findin' a dozen or so more steers so's we kin have us a full load. Lefty, here, has the rail car reserved for Carson City, and it'll be on the siding next Tuesday by four in the mornin'."

Ren grabbed Getwood by his coat lapel and pulled him closer, as he blew his stinking breath on the man while he shouted at him. "Lissen, Get, your ranch's got a real good crop of young beeves that they ain't about to miss fer a spell, an' you'us 'sposed to cut them fence lines near the Caliénte creek so's we could move a few steers a whole lots faster an' easier. I cut that damn fence onest myself, and had one little steer all ready, when all thet hell broke loose."

"Look, Ren, it ain't my fault Hank was on the bluff that day. You were any better shots, there wouldn't have been any slicker opportunity to find more from the main herd gather. It was only about a mile away from the coulee." Getwood continued to rant and rave on and started to turn red in the face.

"'Nother thing," he continued, "I ain't 'bout to be seen any more with the likes of you, until after this deal goes through. I'll meet you at the railroad siding and help load those critters, then I'm on my way to Carson City with the haulin' papers and collect the money. We agree to meet at that abandoned shed on the Dixon property in a week and split the money."

* * *

Mary Anne was at the faro table and extolling her surplus to the patrons while ordering drinks for them with their money. She only appeared to be totally enraptured with the players; she was keeping a good eye on Getwood, just as her close friend, Abbey, asked her to. She strolled to the window and watched as the four men rode out of Walker Lake, separately.

* * *

Aunt Lucy just left with the baby as Hank came to the front of his cabin. He stood at the table on the porch, with the basin, and sloshed some soapy water on his hands and face, before he toweled off and entered.

"Bet you been tendin' that baby all afternoon, sweetheart." Hank spoke to his curvaceous wife with a loving tone, and he held her close, while awaiting her answer.

Abbey kissed Hank with a sensual response and then spoke. "The little fellow has been asleep most of the afternoon, and I just finished giving him his milk before Aunt Lucy came to get him. I'm certain he'll sleep through supper time. Aunt Lucy has a couple of roasting hens in her oven, and we are all going over there for our supper in about another hour, or so."

These were words Hank wanted to hear as he carefully started to remove the plaid shirt Abbey wore with with her tight, denim jeans. She finished removing her own undergarments as Hank deftly divested himself of all his clothing. The peacefulness of their quiet ranch cabin added to the splendor of their passions.

"I love you so much," Abbey whispered to her gallant cowboy.

"You're the finest thing that's ever happened to me, and I'm sure glad I found you that evening in Virginia City. Remember how the gals in your dance troupe were so happy for you? They didn't even know me, and yet, they truly wished us well. Us gettin' hitched-up double to a wagon, was probably the last thing on my mind at that time."

"You're sure talkative, big guy, for a fella' that's been cowboy'n alone all these years. Guess maybe we should have been introduced sooner, so you would have had someone to talk to all this time."

Abbey smiled as she spoke quietly to her young husband, and reached for the quilt to cover her soft back from a draft.

"I suppose actions speak louder than words," he said, as he playfully removed the quilt and quickly smothered her breasts with loving attention from his lips. Abbey started squealing with delight while she lay back nearly exhausted for a moment, before acquiescing to the cowboy's ardent fulfillment.

* * *

The aroma that wafted throughout the victorian-style, main ranch house on the Circle Diamond was created from the kitchen of Aunt Lucy. The roasting chickens were done to the satisfaction of all the family after they all found their places at the dining table.

"You certainly look radiant this evening," Aunt Lucy said to Abbey, as Hank scooted the chair under her and grinned.

"You sure do," Clyde chimed in. "What's the occasion?"

"It's just special being with everyone, and I'm thankful for the privilege of being one of this family. I'm especially happy that you, Cliff, are as resilient as you are. The loss is terrible, but the bliss of Caroline's legacy is truly a blessing. Clay is just your spittin' image, too."

Clifton beamed at the mention of his baby son, and announced to his mother that she was such a good grandmother to Cody. "For that matter, Abbey, I'm just as beholdin' to you for your care and loving attention to my son. Caroline always loved you from the moment Hank showed up here with you at our cow ranch. You became such true friends."

"I know you and Caroline decided the names for a boy child would be Clayton Cody. She told me if it would be a boy, and she was sure it would be, that she was going to call him Clayton, or Clay. Now, you are calling him Cody, is that right?" She asked Clifton.

"I had in mind to call him Cody all along. I think when Colonel Cody starts his wild-west show I'll be able to tell him I honored his name by dubbin' my first boy with it." Everyone laughed at the answer he gave and then his mother announced that she would call the baby Clayton and that's it!

"See you been ridin' the gray mare pretty hard, Getwood," Hank said, next. "She's stocked-up some on her forelegs."

"I had her to town today," Get replied,"I was looking for some new harness pieces, and I didn't want to be late for our supper, like two people I'm a-lookin' at, so, I urged her a mite."

"Don't be runnin' that old mare so much," Clyde said to Getwood, "I want to keep her to jingle-catch the other horses from pasture. Next time, you ride Jiggs."

When the baby went to squalling, after supper, the men lit a shuck for the outside, and left Abbey and Aunt Lucy to clean-up after supper, and the baby.

"Did you talk to Harry Carter any more since you seen him in town with Fern the other day, when he told you 'bout him losin' those five little beeves to those rustlers?" Hank asked Clifton, as they both rolled a smoke.

"Nope," Cliff replied, as the smoke from his hand-rolled 'Bull Durham' lost itself in the gentle, night breeze.

"I do think I'm gonna move those yearlin's tomorrow, from over by Caliénte creek to that pasture west of the Blue Sand mountains."

"Move 'em?" Getwood shouted. "The hell ya' wanna move 'em, for? They's plenty of good grass for them beeves, as well as plenty good water by the creek."

"Getwood, Clifton is right," said Clyde. "Them yearlin's should be a whole lot better off in that pasture by the Blue Sands. You know we're tryin' to market-fatten 'em, and that pasture over there hasn't been grazed since last year."

"There's better mineral content with those grasses, and for sure, there's plenty of our water tanks that are all plumb full by now.

"I'd say go for it, Cliff. I'll ride out with you at first light, and we'll have 'em all settled before evenin' supper, tomorrow. I need to take a respite from some horse breakin' for a spell, and it'll give you a good look at a good horse," Hank reported.

Getwood silently pondered his next move, but, because of a long association, Hank was certain just what it would be.

CHAPTER SIX

THE BLUE SAND
MOUNTAIN SHOOTOUT

The western Nevada weather settled its cold differences during the night, and first light saw Hank and Clifton at the horse barn tacking up their ponies.

"You fixin' to ride ol' Dobie, this mornin', Cliff?" Hank inquired of his cousin. "He's sure a handsome lookin, clay-bank colored, gelding."

"I've not been on him forever three weeks," said Clifton, as he drew up the cinch and adjusted the nose band of the hackamore.

"I'll try to work him easy at first and get the birds outta' his head. He's a good cow horse, you know?"

"Here's couple of cold sandwiches Abbey made for us. Why don't you just stick 'em in your saddle packet?"

"These may come in handy, Hank. Tell Abbey I said thanks."

Getwood rounded the corner of the horse barn on his way to attempt to coax some milk from the tan Guernsey milk cow, when he spied Clifton and Hank.

"Momma asked me to milk ol' Suzie this mornin', 'cause she's messed up tendin' your baby, Clifton. I thought Abbey was gonna do it, 'stead of me. She can jes milk 'er tonight, fer certain, 'cause I got 'bidness' to do."

"I'd like to talk to you about that business. Get, but Cliff and I are headin' out to find those yearlings to pasture," Hank said, "maybe later."

The two cowboy cousins were discussing the Circle Diamond ranch on their search for the gather of heifers at Caliénte creek.

"Was the base for our cow herd on this place when our dads started the operation back in '70?" Hank asked Clifton, as they started down off the ridge together.

"There were mor'n 900 crossbred mama vows, and they brought in mostly the Hereford and Durham mix bulls."

"Yeah, well, I like Uncle Clyde's edict 'bout turnin' the bulls out in May and leavin' 'em until the end of August. They start calving the first of March and we can work the calves in summer, and then make yearlings out of most," Hank sagely replied.

"You know, Hank, if we breed the heifers so they calve a little sooner than the cows, say around the first part of February, we've passed the most of the roughest, high-country, winter weather."

Hank figured this was good herd management, but since they raised only a small amount of hay, they'd supplement the stock to some degree. Especially during the colder periods. "Good thing there's plenty of our sweet water, and enough land to rotate,"

* * *

This time there was no mistaking the three riders, high-tailing it on the east side of the Caliénte creek. There was a good deal of moisture under the piñion pine needles, and the Dobie horse was doing his best to keep his belly pointing downward.

Clifton was coaxing him on, while Hank circled around and got on a rocky shelf where Lawyer found it hard to gain footing on the sand rock plates. When the two cowboys finally got down off the the bluffs and on to some easier flat ground, they took off fast in the direction of the riders.

"Who are they?" Clifton shouted to Hank, as they shouldered the turn-off to the creek together.

"Don't know yet," cried Hank, "but if you spur that clay-bank hard, and I lay on this bay, we can catch 'em before they reach the Blues."

* * *

"Spur thet sorry ol' hoss in the flanks," Ren shouted to Farris, as he and Lefty were leaving the dust behind them.

"This is an old horse, Ren, damn thing ain't got the gall that red-roan of yours has," Farris pleaded.

"You'll wind him fer sure," Lefty hollered. "I'm splittin' off from you boys an I'll see you later at the shack."

Ren thought he'd try for the taller piñons at the base of the Blue Sand, and he reined his speedy red-roan toward a dense thicket, Farris was right behind him.

Ren pulled his saddle rifle from its scabbard as he stepped off his pony, who was sliding to a stop. As Farris approached, Ren reached out and caught the horse's reins and pulled his foreleg under him, and this quickly threw that horse down to the ground.

"T'hell you a-doin', Ren? At's my horse you pulled down. Hell's a-matter witch-ya?'

"Shut up, an' jump on his head 'til I git mah rope on his feet."

"You crazy? them two cowboys' right in front of us . . .t'hell are you a-doin'?"

"These damn piñons ain't big 'nuf to afford us any good protection, an' that ol' horse'll give us some cover to shoot from. Git at it, Farris, an' be quick about it."

Ren had already shouldered his rifle and was firing in the direction of Hank and Clifton, when Farris eventually joined in the shooting.

Only quick thinking by Clifton saved the two cowboys who almost rode into this ambush. He pulled rein the moment he saw the gunfighters ride into the tree line. He signaled Hank, and they were in a flank position, instead of straight in front of those two.

"Can you see 'em, Hank?" said Cliff.

"Yep, there's only two that I can see though," he answered. "There's a horse that looks to be tied down, and I think they are usin' him for cover. Try not to hit him, just aim a little bit higher."

"I can see 'em, plain now, Hank. I'm sure I can hit the guy on the right." Cliff fired three quick shots, and they both heard the man holler out, "I'm hit, Ren, help me." Ren snapped off four or five shots which did pin down the Hall boys for a second or two.

Ren looked quickly over his left shoulder, at his cohort, Farris, and decided instantly that he'd better skedaddle out of that space. He ran fast for the trees where his roan horse was tied, and vaulted to his saddle, and raced toward the slopes of the Blue Sand mountains.

When Hank and Cliff eventually eased past the brush cover and sparse tree outcroppings ahead, they discovered that the firing had stopped and the sounds they heard were coming from the tied-down horse, who was fighting his rope-tied castings.

The closer they both crawled, the more cautious they became until Hank came upon Farris who was sprawled over the side of his prone pony, and gasping for breath.

Hank grabbed the wounded man and pulled him to the side, while securing his rifle and his six-gun. Clifton quickly cut the foot ropes and the neck rope from the downed horse, and jumped back out of the way.

"What d'ya suppose prompted these men to run from us and then shoot at us like this?" Cliff remarked to Hank.

"These bozos are part of the cattle thieving' that's been goin' on in this county for some time, Cliff, and now we've finally caught us a live one." Hank said this before realizing the man in his arms was but barely alive. "Hold on there, mister, we need some answers."

Clifton, returning to the spot after a quick search for tracks leading away, said, "whoever it is sure lit out fast. Looks like he didn't care much for his partner at any rate. How's he doin', anyway?"

"Hey, you!" Hank spoke loud and very clear to the rustler who was dying. "Who are you, and who's behind all this mess?"

"R-Ren M-Morgan," the rustler gasped, "it's him and his brother-in-law, Lefty, that's who, and that pal of Lefty's, (gasp), he knowed from prison, he's the . . .(cough) . . . oohuuh."

"Wal," Clifton said, "it sounds like that's his last breath. Reckon we'd better get his body to the sheriff, and tell him just what happened. Help me strap him on that ol' horse, and I'll lead him, Hank."

* * *

Deputy Peabody re-tipped his chair forward on the planking by the front door to the town jail, as he followed the movements of the two riders. They were leading a crippled, black horse with a body draped over the saddle.

"Oh, howdy Clifton, didn't recognize Hank's bay horse or the clay-bank you're a-ridin'. Lookin' fer the doc or the sheriff?"

"Where's Jim?" Cliff inquired.

"Sheriff's in Virginia City," the deputy answered. He should be back later this afternoon. What can I do fer ya? Who'zat?"

"Well, I s'pose we got to fill out some papers pertainin' to this bad hombré here," Cliff remarked. Hank's purty sure this is one of the gang that's been rustlin' the beeves in this county, of late. There were three of 'em when we seen 'em, and we chased them to an area where they nearly ambushed us."

"We exchanged for a while," Hank explained quickly. "We managed to nick this one. Problem is, he died on us and the others high-tailed it."

"Any idea who he is, Peabody?" Cliff asked the deputy.

"Naw, but I'll check the posters in the office and maybe when the sheriff comes back from Virginia City, he'll be have an idea. Meantime, I reckon I'd best fetch the mortician. Could you boys lead the horse with the body to the parlor whilst you still got him tied horseback?"

"We'll accommodate you, Peabody," Hank said, as he pursed to his horse, "but Cliff and I got some yearlings to pasture, so we've not got all day."

* * *

Clifton and Hank quick-stepped their ponies as they headed from Walker Lake in the direction of Caliénte creek. It wasn't yet high noon and they thought they still had time to complete their chore.

"Here's one of those sandwiches, Hank," Clifton said, as he unwrapped his and one for his cousin. "By the time we finish movin' those yearlings it'll likely be dark, and after supper time when we get home."

"We gotta find 'em and gather 'em first, you know," Hank chuckled his reply.

About an hour later, the two Circle Diamond cowboys came across a herd of yearling steers and tallied thirty-eight. This included a couple of 'moss-back' cows that joined in the cut.

It took almost three hours to prod these cattle to their destination, which was about ten miles from where they had found them.

They arrived at the section on their range that they wanted to graze the beeves. It had a natural represso that held a great amount of water, and it was full. A copious amount of scrub brush grew near the base on the side of the foothills of the Blue Sand mountains. It also had a good crop of second-year short-grass and an abundance of prickly-pear cactus, too.

A mixture of piñon pine smoke mixed with mesquite was curling from the chimney of the main house as Hank and Clifton rode into the barn. The aroma encircled the as they put up their ponies and headed for the ranch house.

. . . . A DISCOVERY . . . .

Clyde, and Ranger, his faithful dog, heard the men ride in, and met them at the barn.

"You must have had some problems with them there yearlin's, boys, else you'd been in a-fore darkness," Clyde spoke, while he handed Hank a lantern.

"Well, Dad, we've got a heap more to tell you about today's circle-ride, but first, We're headin' for Ma's supper table," Cliff answered.

The supper tasted mighty good to the two hungry cowboys, and the beef roast that Aunt Lucy fixed was nearly totally consumed.

Clifton was about to inform everyone of the events that happened to them today, when Hank interrupted him with a statement that was directed to Getwood.

"Hey, Get, we found a man on the trail today that had been shot from his black horse, and when Cliff and I got to him, he named a man called Ren." Cliff was astounded at the dispense of the truth, but he decided to play out the hand and listen to the rest of the story.

"Now, whut'er you tellin' me this for? I don't know no hombré by that name." Getwood braced himself as he looked first to his dad and then over to his mother, before he confronted Cliff and Hank. "Whut's thet got to do with them cows you'us a-lookin' fer?"

"Well, plenty, Getwood," Hank spoke up. "We took his body to Walker Lake to get some identity on him, but the sheriff was in Virginia City, and the deputy was no help."

"Hank!" Abbey cried out, "what are . . ."

"Not now, honey," Hank retorted.

Aunt Lucy looked stunned, but Clyde, wise in the ways of events that suddenly occur, re-assured her with a few words of comfort.

"Let Cliff continue," he said, smoothly.

The two cow punchers had not yet revealed a word of any gun battle that had involved them. Clifton didn't want to worry his mother, so he refrained from saying he and Hank were involved with any shooting.

"When we picked this feller up from him bein' shot, he managed to name another man, and was about to reveal a third, when he just upped and died. Hank thinks this bunch is the rustlers that been stealin' all the cows, lately."

Getwood suddenly spoke. "What was the name of the other feller that he said?"

He paled when Hank said - "Lefty."

Momentarily there was silence, and then Getwood said, "Well, er - thet there name don't ring no bell with me, neither."

"Just thought you might have heard of these men, Get. I know how much you're interested in us catching any rustlers, and just how much you'd like to help," Hank said, with his tongue in his cheek as he slowly glanced over at Abbey, who averted her eyes. Clifton pushed his chair back and stood while asking his mom if he could visit with Cody, or was he still asleep?

"Little Clayton has been fed and he's still asleep, but he'll awaken soon. I'll change him and you can entertain him 'til he's ready to go back to his little crib for the night," Cliff's mom stated.

"I'm sorta tired , Ma, but I'm sure gonna have some fun with him, anyway. "

* * *

The moon was hiding itself behind some clouds as they walked in their cabin. Abbey quickly turned and bolted the door before she confronted her tall, handsome husband.

"Hank, you tell me everything, right now, and from the beginning. I have a right to know."

"Sweetheart, I'm just not positive yet, but I sure do suspect Getwood is in cahoots with a gang of cow thieves. He's been hiding something, and Uncle Clyde and Cliff are about to decide the same as me about Getwood."

Abbey carefully maneuvered her lithe body to the side of the bed, where she sat upright to pose a statement to Hank.

"Certainly, Aunt Lucy doesn't really suspect anything, what makes you so suspicious?"

Hank slowly proceeded to tell Abbey all about the fight he had with Getwood, and the real and true outcome of what happened to the old jingle horse, Brownie.

Hank went on to explain how he'd seen two of the rustlers ride away from the ranch one morning, and that he recognized a red-roan horse as the one he'd seen trying to run off a steer at Caliénte creek, and then he saw that same horse again, today. "Why are you smiling'?" Hank asked his beautiful wife, when he looked into her hazel eyes.

"I've been reading you like a book, sweetheart," she said, "but, until now, I haven't been able to put it all together, so I shared a woman's thoughts with Mary Anne. She's been keeping tabs on Getwood, when he goes into town in Walker Lake. She also told me that he meets with some very dangerous men, one of whom she knows.

I think she said his name was Farris."

CHAPTER SEVEN

TIME TO MAKE DECISIONS

Abbey was writhing in ecstasy as the gentle strength of his legs wrapped her in a locked embrace, while they passionately kissed each other' bodies. His fingers ran through her auburn colored tresses.

She softly and fervently pulled his head to reach her wet lips. The impetuous approach of Abbey's gorgeous, lithe body, enraptured Hank's tender feelings toward his greatest possession.

His memories turned back pages in his time book to reveal the reasons for desiring this goddess, and his total commitment to loving her for an eternity.

Breakfast, that Abbey fixed them this morning, was not half over when Clyde's dog. Ranger, started to the front room of the ranch house. he only growled slightly, as Clyde looked through the curtains hanging on the window at the heavy, oak-solid, front door.

"Howdy, Jim," Clyde spoke, waving at the sheriff to tie-off his horse and come inside. "You're just in time for some of Abbey's flap jacks, and coffee. Come on in and take your seat here . . . Ranger, go lie down."

"G'mornin', Lucille, and miss Abbey. Seein' both you ladies is always worth the ride over here. 'Mornin', boys," the sheriff said, "I'm obliged to you for some bait, the ride was a little dusty. Understand you got a good calf crop, Clyde. I know how hard you all have been workin', and the word is your ranch is sure garner'n a good reputation for bein' the best, as well as the biggest, in the county."

The sheriff went on. "Well, I guess I haven't seen you since Caroline's funeral, Cliff, and I know how much you miss her. After this fine breakfast, I would be mighty gratified to see the button you named Cody."

"You just set right there, Sheriff Sager, I'll fetch little Clayton, and you can see for your-self what a spitting image he is of his daddy," Lucille said, as she scurried to the baby's room. Cliff beamed again, and poured syrup all over the table.

Getwood politely asked his mother if she'd excuse him from the table, as soon as he saw the sheriff come inside, saying that he'd better see to the milk cow, in case the baby was wanting some milk. He surreptitiously glanced at everyone at the table, but avoided Hank's eyes, as he took his leave through the kitchen exit.

* * *

The day was greeting some high wind gusts, as the men walked toward the corrals and rolled a smoke, and picked their teeth, after the meal.

"Peabody told me all he could about the mess you boys got yourselves into yesterday," Jim Sager said to Hank and Clifton. "I tried to find some information on that dead hombré you brought in, but nothin' came of it. 'Fraid I'm gonna have to hold you both on maybe a suspicion of murder char. . ."

"Hold on, Jim, you know full well that lead poisoning was all self defense," Hank interrupted the sheriff.

"Sorry, boys, but I'm duty-bound to arrest you on this charge. Seein' Clyde's a close friend and Lucille'd worry too much, I'll just hold you, Hank. Reckon Cliff can take care of the ranch and the women folks."

"You sure you can't reconsider a bit, Jim? You're not positive exactly how that puncher was shot, and I don't believe you can prove anything under the circumstances the way they are right now." Hank requested.

"There's a series of events a-leadin' up to this, Jim," Clifton interjected.

"These men have to be the ones rustlin' cows in Mineral county. It'd help if you knew the name of the dead man. We already know the name of the two rustlers now, and near 'bout found out who's likely the leader."

"Well, boys, Abe Klein's our county attorney and he advised me last night that you two may be on to something, so I may not arrest you just yet. I aim to ride back to town and try to find out more about this Ren Morgan feller, and also the one they called Lefty."

Sheriff Jim Sager whistled sharply, and his horse unloosed his rein at the hitch post by the house, and started for the sheriff at the barn.

"Sorry I worried you boys. However, I had to know just what you had to say."

* * *

Getwood had his mind made up not to meet with his gang until after the train car with the rustled cattle was loaded, and delivered and paid for, but the shooting of Farris changed things. He decided to ride to Walker Lake. This time he saddled Jiggs, instead of the gray mare.

Get figured this would please his 'Pap', be-sides, Jiggs was a gelding, and he preferred geldings over mares. He reined his horse at the Lucky Partner saloon, and then ordered a bottle of whisky when he entered.

Getwood was nervously fondling the glass with some whisky in it, when Mazie came down from upstairs with a partially drunken cowboy following her. When he spied Getwood, he plopped himself at the table and he hollered for Mazie to bring him a glass.

"What'r-you-doin' here, Boyle?" Lefty shouted at the top of his voice. "I didn't think I'd see you 'til we got to the shack."

"Keep your voice down, Lefty, and don't use that name again, ever!" Getwood sneered as he snapped at his inebriated acquaintance. "I got news fer ya', an hit ain't good. Ren has gone and shot Farris!"

"Th-hell you talkin' 'bout? I jes left 'em at the Blue Sands. We located some beeves and your family boys jumped us. We all lit a shuck and Farris was havin' a hard time keepin' up with his black pony, an' I told 'em we should split us apart. I never had any i-dee that Ren would gun down Farris - don't make no sense to me."

"Well," Getwood said, "them two boys told me they come on ol' Farris' body and his black horse, an' tuk 'em to the sheriff in Walker Lake. They claimed they didn't know who he was, but they said he named you an' Ren as partners."

"D-did you say they named me? How'd they know that unless Farris told 'em afore he died. Did he say that Ren gunned him down?"

"I don't know, Lefty, but you'd best sober up and ride outta here quick as you can, if'n the sheriff comes and finds us, it would turn into a big mess."

"S-ssay, Get," Mary Anne hissed, walking to the table where Lefty just departed, "where's your fried going in such an all-fired hurry? Was it something that Mazie said to him?"

"N-no, it's that he just found out a friend of his was gunned down by Lefty's own brother-in-law, an' he needs to find out what happened." he then guzzled down his glass full of whisky.

"I'll bet the sheriff would sure be interested in talking to Lefty. He's likely looking for the man that shot his friend," Mary Anne said, coyly. "Did you know who the man was, the man that was shot?"

"O'course not! Whut makes you think I did?"

"Oh, I don't know. I thought it may be one of the men I saw you drinking with in here the other week. Mazie told me that Deputy Peabody told her they were trying to find the name of the dead man, but no one has claimed the body. Maybe you should give the sheriff the names of the men you were with."

Mary Anne was delighted with the appalling expression on Getwood's face. "Oh, are you leaving, Getwood? You haven't finished all of the bottle yet?"

His thoughts were on the sorry outcome of what had happened to Farris, and what Lefty and Ren were going to do next. Getwood needed them to rustle enough of the Circle Diamond steers to fill out the train carload to Carson City. Get talked to himself while he rode out.

* * *

Sheriff Sager entered the Lucky Partner saloon just after he had his lunch at the Palace Hotel dining room. He made his way to the Faro table and asked Mary Anne and Mazie for a minute if their time.

"My deputy tells me that you two may know who the dead man is that's over at the undertaker's parlor. Would you walk over there with me if I asked you kindly?"

"'Course we will Jim," said Mary Anne. "She and I know most of the buckaroos that drift into our place, usually one way or another."

Twenty minutes later, the sheriff had a name to go with the body.

"Holden Farris," Mary Anne said. "I saw him with Lefty and Getwood, and a fourth man, several times, at least, in the saloon."

Mazie spoke up, saying, "Lefty is one of the men. Lefty Barker. Him and I meet on, uh - on occasion, he says his wife don't really understand him, and anyway, he ain't seen her in a spell. Don't ask me who the other one is, but I've seen 'em all in the Lucky Partner."

"If I'm not mistaken, Sheriff, I think Lefty's wife has a brother that used to run with him now and again. I'll bet he's the other one, besides Getwood," Mary Anne stated.

"Thanks, ladies," the sheriff said. You've been a good help. I think I'll telegraph Carson City to see if they have any more information."

As the two saloon gals walked back to the Lucky Partner, Mary Anne related to Mazie an earlier statement made to her from Getwood.

"It just now came to me! I asked him why your friend, Lefty, was in such a hurry to leave after - uh, your visit. He told me he informed Lefty that a man we know now as Farris, was gunned down by Lefty's brother-in-law, and that Hank and Clifton told Get all about it. Getwood knows who Lefty's brother-in-law is, and when I told Getwood he should tell the sheriff, he just up and left, too."

"Mazie, something's up. Getwood's scared."

"How does Get fit in all this big mess?"

"Not sure, but now I am sure the sheriff knows more than he's tellin.'"

* * *

"G'wan an' take him, Uncle Clyde he's broke good now, and a pure pleasure to ride," Hank said, as he handed the reins of the horse to the old rancher.

"You've been wantin' to see that good crop of yearlings Cliff and I just moved to that pasture, over by the Blue Sands."

"I guess I should give ol' Lawyer a try, I've been admiring him ever' since we got him, and you've done a fine job of gentlin' him for an old man to get on and enjoy."

Clyde Hall was tall in the saddle, as he forked the big bay horse.

"C'mon, Ranger," he said to his trusty dog, as the three of them started off across a section of the Circle Diamond ranch.

CHAPTER EIGHT

A SAD DISCOVERY

A high-powered rifle shot out of the late afternoon sun, knocked the life from Clyde and spilled him from Lawyer's saddle.

There was no awakening. The bullet entered his back, struck a rib, and went right into his heart.

Ranger was beside himself. He tugged at the body, pulled it away from the trail, whined and cried, and finally lay down next to his worshipful pal. Almost immediately, the bay horse trotted off toward his home corral, leaving Ranger alone with his beloved friend and master.

Lefty was certain he'd fatally hit the rider on the big bay horse. He recognized Hank Hall's horse from afar, and knew that Ren and Getwood would be pleased at his true resourcefulness. He turned away off the high bluff, above the flat mesa, and continued to ride in the direction of the Blue Sands, and the lush pasture beyond.

Approaching from the south, a single rider crossed the wash and circled the mesa. It was Getwood in his determination to seek out those yearlings he knew his step-brother and Hank moved from Caliénte creek. He felt certain that Ren and Lefty would try again to rustle enough of these cattle to make the train-car load.

* * *

Orange and crimson were the colors involved with the cerulean blue of the evening winter sky. Lucy and Abbey were taking turns fixing the evening meal, and trading off playing with a happy, healthy baby boy.

"Here's a few more logs for the fireplace," Clifton remarked, as he entered the house with both arms full of cut wood. "I imagine Dad and Getwood will be ridin' in 'bout now for supper. It's a tad late for fixin' the pump at the wind mill wash. I guess they'll both be in soon."

Hank was washing up at the basin on the front porch, before he entered the ranch house.

"Ahh, Cliff, I see you're finally gettin' to play with young Cody. He sure is a button. Where's Uncle Clyde?"

"Not in yet, Hank. Reckon I ought to check the barn," Cliff said, as he gave his son over to it's grandma's loving arms. Both cowboys were worried that Clyde wasn't home yet. Hank felt maybe he should not have insisted that his uncle ride the new horse, although the old rancher was as adept as anyone his age; more than most at any age.

No sooner than they turned the corner of the corral, they heard the horse first, then saw him. It was Lawyer, panting, with one rein broken and the other dragging. No one was in the saddle.

"My God," exclaimed Clifton,"somethin' fearsome happened to Dad, and I'll bet ol' Ranger is still with him."

* * *

The red-orange sky turned gray over Lefty and his paint horse as they rode off the bluff, where the rifle shot originated. He swept past the outcropping of rocks, and white sage, and a few Joshua trees. All at once a trail merged, and Lefty jerked hard on his pony to avert the rush of a sorrel horse heading at a very sharp angle toward him.

"Boyle!, I-I mean, Getwood! What t'hell you a-doin' outchere?"

"Been fixin' the pump out at Windmill Wash, and I was a-headin' home when I seen your dust and a spotted pony . . .figured it was you. What are you doin' here?" Get asked Lefty as he pulled rein and slid off the back of Jiggs.

"Lissen, you ain't a-gonna believe this, but I jist now shooted thet smart-ass cousin o'yourn, plumb off'n his bay horse! I'll bet thet shot was over 200 yards, and it gittin' darker by the minute. They's nobody, 'ceptin' you, within miles of this'ere place, so ain't no way of anybody knowin' nuthin' 'bout any of this." Lefty was still grinning and belching, from the dregs of his liquor canteen he carried.

""Wul, now, ain't this a very merry Christmas? How t'hell'd you know it was Hank Hall? Did ya kill him, sure 'nuf?" Getwood was ecstatic awaiting Lefty's confirmation.

"They's no question 'bout it. I seen thet big ol' bay of his too many times to ever mistake it. Now we got clear sailin' with them yearlin's. I seen the tracks they made a-comin' to water. They ain't so very far away."

The two men rode the trail a ways together, while discussing their separate destinations.

"Wait'll I find Ren and tell him what happened this evening," Lefty clucked, "He'll have to pay me a lot more mind now."

"I've got to ride hard to get to the ranch in time for supper. My brother knows I was to be fixin' the mill pump. I'll tell him I had to go to town first to get some parts for the pump, and I'll meet you and Ren at the Dixon property the day after tomorrow. They won't know what's happened to their pet cowboy, and they'll figure he was probably gonna stay in town. Anyway, I'll be back there tomorrow if they want me for anything, so you and Ren's got to ketch all them yearlin's first thing tomorrow, and brand 'em."

"We still got us a couple of days afore thet rail car will be at the siding. I'm sure I'll find Ren at the Lucky Partner, so I'm off fer there, rat now. Oh, . . .I sure am sorry 'bout your damn cousin." Lefty just laughed, when he waved and parted company.

* * *

Abbey was uncomfortable with the absence of Hank and Clifton, who had earlier walked to the barn and left her with Aunt Lucy, to take care of Cody and get supper on the table. Abbey was at the door when Clifton and Hank came running toward the house in a great hurry.

* * *

When Lefty arrived in Walker Lake he headed straight for the Lucky Partner saloon. He tied off his paint horse at the hitch rail next to the red-roan that he knew was Ren's horse. Pushing past a gaggle of half-sober miners and a few carefree buckaroos crowding the bar, Lefty spied Ren at the back card table.

Ren had just risen from the table to use the outhouse when Lefty bumped into him. Ren was so full of whisky he failed to immediately recognize Lefty, and threw a punch at the man who was blocking his pathway.

"Outta' my way," Ren slurred, as he stepped over his unrecognized accomplice. Lefty got up mad but unhurt, and followed Ren to the outhouse behind the saloon.

"I need to know why you up and kilt Farris. Whut happened when we split off from them Hall boys? Dammit, Ren, come outer there, we gots to talk." Lefty was demanding his brother-in-law answer him.

Several moments later, Ren emerged from the half-moon doorway and confronted Lefty in a more sober condition.

"I never shot ol' Farris, dumb-butt. After you split off, him and I made a stand in the trees, and them two cowboys shot him. I peeled outta there so quick, they never knew who else was there. I lost 'em when I found an old Piaute trail through the mountains.

"What made you think I shot Farris, anyway?"

"Boyle . . uh, Getwood Hall told me. Said that's whut his brother told to him. Anyways, lissen', Have I got great news for you!"

* * *

"Something's dreadfully wrong, Hank! You two are in an awful hurry." Abbey gasped, as she watched her lean husband strap on his gun holster. Clifton grabbed an extra box of cartridges from the drawer, and his gun, too.

"I'm taking this extra reata," Hank told Cliff, as he coiled and tied it.

"What is it? What's happening?" Aunt Lucy asked, as she entered the room with her arms full of little Clayton.

"Papa may be hurt, Momma. He was ridin' Hank's bay horse, Lawyer, and the ol' horse just came into the barn . . .alone."

Summoning all her courage, Aunt Lucy remained calm, as she attempted to reinforce a positive outlook with everyone present.

"If Ranger is with him, I'm certain he'll be all right. You boys be careful. I just know you'll find him . . .and find him safe and sound."

"I never should have let him ride the Lawyer," Hank said, regretfully.

"Nonsense," Aunt Lucy replied. "He's fallen off more horses in his lifetime than you've ever seen, Hank, dear. Now, you two just go find him soon as you can."

"Abbey," Cliff spoke, "when Getwood rides in, tell him what's happened. He'll want to ride out to look for Dad, also. Now, don't worry Mom, Abbey, we'll find him."

"I'm ridin' ol' Buster, Abbey. He's a great night horse, and he's stout enough to carry double. So long." Hank bid farewell.

* * *

"You ain't messin' with me, are you, Lefty?" Has my little ol' brother-in-law actually done away with that damned buckaroo?"

"You bet, Ren. I done good, right?" Lefty grinned, showing Ren the seven teeth he had left, as the spittle ran from the corner of his bearded face. "I crossed trail with Getwood Hall as he was a-headin' fer his own ranch, and I told him about the shot that I made."

"He was sure 'nuf proud, and said if I was to see you tonight, to be sure to tell you where them yearlin's was, and fer us to gather 'em jist as soon's we can."

"Let's get outta this damn cold and get us another drink. I jist need to git warm," Ren interrupted.

Lefty never skipped a beat. "We can put 'em with all the rest in Miller Canyon. Getwood said he'd probably stay at the ranch on account of all the grief that'd pile up when the family found out about that there 'precious cowboy' of theirs, gettin' kilt . . . Jeasous, Ren, d'jew ever see the body on thet woman of his'n? She's . . .

"You got diarrhea of the mouth, boy. Don't you never shut up?" Ren wondered aloud. Now, let's get us a drink for the chill of the night, and decide about them yearlin's for tomorrow. You best take both our hosses over to the livery, we're gonna room here tonight."

"I'll do it in a minute, Ren. Ah, . . soon's as I find where Mazie is, an' save me some of thet bottle, too."

"Yeah! Well, whar's Ruthie?" belched Ren, holding up the bottle.

(. . . THERE . . . ON THE ROAD WAY . . .)

It was dusk and the temperature dropped when the sun finally faded behind the Wassuk mountains. The moon wasn't yet fully exposing itself when Hank unsaddled Lawyer, inspecting him, then put him in one of the barn stalls, and tossed him a rake-full of hay.

Clifton hurriedly tacked-up Dobie, his clay-bank colored horse, and flipped a rope on Buster, who was in the far corral with several of a string of horses. "Here's your good, night horse, Hank. Hurry, now - we have to get ridin', and we're losin' time."

"We likely should head straight for our west pasture where we put the cut of yearlings. I'm certain Uncle Clyde wanted to ride out to have a look at them," Hank announced.

Hank was trying hard to read a sign of Lawyer's hoof prints on the trail.

"Never mind the tracks," said Cliff, we'll just cross the road to the pasture area. That's bound to be the direction he took.

"Over there!," shouted Hank, as the moon openly shone from behind a cloud bank. "On the road-way! See it?"

"You bet!," exclaimed Cliff. They both quickly peeled off the top and slid their ponies down the steep embankment from the mesa to-ward the road.

Ranger was barking and circling with his tail tucked, when the two cowboys both pulled rein and dismounted.

The wind that came with the clearing night on this section of the Circle Diamond was as piercing as the dagger that found its mark in Clifton's heart. Ranger was attempting to lick both their faces while they gently turned Clyde's body, vainly searching for just any signs of life.

Hank was the first to discover it. "Cliff, look at this." He was cradling Clyde from a seated position on the ground. "He never had a chance. He's been shot in the back, and from a distance, too."

"Dammit, dammit!" Cliff shouted, as he stepped nearer. "What in the world has happened? Who-n'hell would shoot a gentle old man in the back? For God's sake, Hank, what's goin' on?" Clifton Hall was absolutely devastated, as he queried his cowboy cousin.

It was extremely difficult for Cliff to accept the fact that his father had been ambushed. He truly was expecting to find him with, at the worst, a few bones broken from a fall from the 'Lawyer' horse.

"I've known a lot of great cowboys, and your daddy could top the list. We've both been blessed with a legacy from this man." Hank sadly related.

"I just can't figure why anyone would want to shoot my father," Clifton replied, "unless some-one was jealous of all his holdings."

"I think I've figured it out, Cliff. Whoever killed your dad wasn't after him at all." Hank said, while he lifted his Uncle Clyde across the saddle of Buster, his ol' brown, night-horse. "C'mon, Ranger, let's go break the news to the family." He leaned across his saddle and said to his cousin, "Hang in there, Cliff."

CHAPTER NINE

A JOURNEY IN HARSH WEATHER

A quarter moon lit the cold night as Getwood rode the last few miles home to the Circle Diamond ranch. He put Jiggs up in the corral, after he'd wiped him down and tossed him some alfalfa hay. He made his way to the porch at the main house and saw Abbey standing in the doorway.

"I'm a little late," he said, as he reached for the basin and soap on the porch table.

"You may want to ride back out again, Getwood," Abbey said. She was standing sideways, leaning against the jamb of the door, and silhouetted by back-lighting from the glow of the fire burning cozy and warm.

"H-huh? W-whazzat?" Getwood's jaw was as slack as a grass rope on a rainy day. He stood, mouth agape, looking at the curving outline of Abbey's comely torso.

"I said, you may want to ride out to look for your dad. Clyde was riding Hank's horse, Lawyer, earlier this evening, and about an hour ago the horse came back to the barn without Uncle Clyde. The boys have lef . . ."

"Did you say Lawyer," he shouted, y-you mean h-he came to the barn . . .h-he . . .Pap was ridin' him? It was supposed to b-be . . ."

Jiggs was visibly spent, so Getwood slapped a saddle on ol' Croppy, a big sorrel horse from Montana that had both the tips of his ears frozen, and spurred hard to leave the ranch. He was blindly riding toward Walker Lake, and his thoughts were as scrambled as his conscious.

How could that dense bastard, Lefty, make such a stupid mistake, Get thought to himself. Even if he recognized the bay horse he should never have shot, 'til he was sure.

"'Pears ol' Lefty jist wanted to get even with Hank and Cliff for them shootin' at him, and Ren and Farris," he said outloud to the crop-eared horse he was hustling into town.

"Hell," he shouted, "I'll bet that damn Ren never shot Farris at all. I'll bet it was Hank, or my brother done it. Now look whut its come down to." Getwood had no intention of looking for his father. He would leave that up to his step-brother and Hank. He wasn't even thinking of his mother at this point.

About all that was on Get's mind was to find his 'gang', get the cattle all moved, the brands changed, and shipped and paid for.

He tried to formulate, in his mind, just how he would arrange the sale and payment for the cattle when he got them to the stockyards in Carson City, Nevada.

Getwood arrived in Walker Lake and surprised himself by riding past the Lucky Partner. He was on his way to the livery stable at the end of town.

"Wake up, Hiram," he yelled. "This damn stable has got to keep open all hours, jist the same as the hotel does."

Hiram McCoy stumbled from his cot in the tack room at the livery to the aisle way that led to the barn stalls.

"Who the hell's out there?" the caretaker sleepily said, as he hoisted his lantern higher above his head. "It's the middle of the night, ya know?"

"Need you to rub this horse down and put him up 'til mornin'," Getwood answered.

Hiram mumbled something to himself after he recognized the horse as one he once owned, before his brother, Stubby, sold him to the Circle Diamond ranch." Didn't recognize you at first, I'll take care of ol' Croppy, but it'll cost you a dollar more for the disturbance. Where are you a-goin', to the Palace Hotel?"

"I'm lookin' fer Ren Morgan, or fer Lefty Barker," Getwood growled, to the sleepy groom.

"There was a big card game at the saloon after supper," Hiram said to Getwood. "It's likely still a-goin' on, an I reckon they're both a-playin' in that game."

Getwood was upset as he made his way over to the dram house. He knew he better find his gang and make certain they catch those yearlings and move them to Miller Canyon before first light this morning.

He still didn't know how he'd react or what he'd say to Lefty when he confronted him for the awful mistake he made when he shot Clyde Hall. He decided that after he saw the gang, he would hurriedly ride home and they'd feel he'd been searching for his step-father.

* * *

Hank was sitting behind the cantle on Buster's hips with his Uncle Clyde's body carefully draped over the leather saddle. The two cowboys were a very disconsolate duo, riding into the ranch yard.

They gently wrapped the body in a blanket and tarpaulin before they put it in the back of the spring-board wagon.

Hank hitched the team, while Clifton went to get two lanterns to hang on the wagon for their journey into Walker Lake.

Ranger jumped into the wagon and lay down beside the body of his beloved master. No amount of coaxing would move him away. Aunt Lucy appeared in the doorway on the porch at the house, with Abbey following her.

"Mom, stay there," Clifton instructed, as he reached the steps in front. "It's Daddy. . . we found him just off the road around the mesa over by the Blue Sands."

"H-he's - not - alive, is he, Clifton?" his mother queried, as she reached for Abbey to steady her, at once.

"I'm so sorry Mother. H-he's been shot."

"Oh, no, no," she cried, while she tried to regain her composure. "W-why? Who?" She was trying to seek answers she didn't really want told. Abbey was trying to comfort her as well, and so was Hank, in an awkward moment.

Clifton sat with his mother for a spell, back inside, on the sofa by the fireside. After a time, Abbey brought the baby in the room and placed him in Aunt Lucy's loving arms. By so doing, this seemed to bring things more into perspective.

* * *

Clifton drove the team into town with his father's body, and Hank rode along on a young horse from the cavvy he'd been breaking. It was about two o'clock in the morning, and turning colder each moment. The men wanted to get the body to the funeral director and make all the arrangements, to spare Aunt Lucy the task.

It started with a fierce, desert dust-swirl-ing wind storm. The cold weather and the moisture the wind blew in, caused blizzard conditions and it developed a snow storm that befell the men and the wagon.

The lanterns were almost useless, for the snow that fell was so heavy, it blotted any available light. The team worked hard to fight the side-blowing snow that fell, and Cliff was doing the best that he could to keep the team working and as calm as possible.

The road to town was obliterated, and Hank forced his pony out front to search out all the landmarks he remembered.

The men figured it was still three or four miles before they would reach Walker Lake, and at the rate they were going that could mean at least, two more hours before they'd arrive.

At last, a tall, wooden junction signpost appeared almost in front of them indicating the outskirts of the town of Walker Lake.

Daylight would arrive late because the snowstorm's darkness prevailed. Nearly a foot of snow fell on the road to town, and the bone-chilling effect it had on the two was evident as they miraculously reined-in the sorrel team at McCoy's Livery, and shook the white mantle from themselves. Ranger crawled out from the tarpaulin in the wagon bed and jumped down.

* * *

Aunt Lucy could hardly bear to watch as Hank and her son departed in the wagon with her husband of almost fifty years. Abbey had little Cody in her arms now, and she was ushering Lucy inside and away from the cruel cold of the night.

"Come back to the warm fire and relieve your chill, Aunt Lucy, and let me get you a shot or two of whisky."

"Well . . .I'd rather not. Only our sweet baby can comfort me now, Abbey, dear."

She gathered the child in her arms and made her way to the fireside rocker and said, "Oh, Clayton, your grand dad loved you so very much. He just couldn't wait for you to grow some, so he'd be able to teach . . ."

"Aunt Lucy, I know it helps to talk about him, and share any experiences you've endured," Abbey interrupted. Especially when it has to do with any of both of your thoughts of little Clay."

"I just can't imagine why anyone would want to take his life," Lucille said about her dear husband, as she fought back tears that rolled down her cheeks.

"Oh, Getwood isn't back from his search for his father, and he has no way of knowing of Clyde's awful fate."

The snow at the Circle Diamond cow ranch was deepening as the early morning crept in.

Abbey returned from her next door cabin after freshening herself and starting a fire in their fireplace to abate the chill.

"I'll fix some breakfast, Aunt Lucy, while you're holding Clayton."

"You know, Getwood still isn't home, and he'll be starved as well as near frozen when he does arrive," Lucille was commiserating.

* * *

Meanwhile, Getwood slugged through the drifted snow at the back end of the livery, and bade goodbye to the two drunken members he'd threatened to shoot if they didn't do as he outlined. They were already late on their journey to the pasture where the yearling cattle were.

The drifting snow caused no less a problem than sobering them for their task. Get was certain the bitter cold would clear their heads and ready them for the job to be done. He would meet them on Tuesday, to begin to load.

* * *

"Well, I see your brother is in town, Cliff," Hiram said, as he helped put up the sorrel team and transfer the long, tarpaulin-wrapped object to the long bench inside.

"Getwood? Here?" Clifton said, surprised, as he quickly looked at Hank, who had already noticed ol' Croppy over in the second stall.

"Yup," Hiram mused. "Come in the middle of the night, lookin' fer two fellers who he sa..."

"Well, howdy, Get." Hank interrupted Hiram, when he spoke to the man entering the back side of the stable and stomping snow from his body and boots.

"Guess you need to know some very sad news."

"I already know my dad's missing. I been all over a-lookin' fer his tracks, way a-fore the storm hit, and figured he maybe drifted into town just this . . ."

"He's dead, Getwood." Clifton said, as he confronted his step-brother in the aisle-way of Hiram McCoy's livery stable.

CHAPTER TEN

A STABLE ESCAPE

A petulant smirk appeared on the face of Getwood, when he attempted to react surprised at Clifton's announcement that Clyde was dead.

"I really expected a more shocked emotion from you, Get. You almost act as if you already knew Daddy was dead." Clifton remarked.

"N-no, no, I don't know nuthin'. When I rode into the ranch Abbey told me that my father was ridin' your damn bay horse, Hank, and the horse came back here without him. I saddled up ol' Croppy, 'cause Jiggs was used up and I went out lookin' fer him. But I don't have any idea who shot him."

"Hold on, Getwood," Hank said. "Just what makes you think Uncle Clyde was shot and killed? Cliff never said he was murdered, he might-a fell off and got killed."

"W-well, uh, I-I jist must've heered it from somebody . . .uh, Abbey told me. Yeah, that's it! Abbey told me when . . ."

"She said no such thing, and you know it," Hank fumed. "Abbey only knew the horse came in without Uncle Clyde, unless you got eagle wings and snow shoes, and been to the ranch and back here, since we left with your dad's body. Tell him, Clyde!"

"Hank's right. What more do you know about this whole thing? And just what're you doin' here?"

* * *

Outside the livery stable the sun sure was gaining on the clouds, as the morning grew older. Townsfolk were busy digging the snow drifts from the planked sidewalks and steps, to allow passage to the business establishments, and especially to the Lucky Partner saloon.

Hank and Cliff were debating on whether to take Getwood with them to the sheriff's office, or one of them fetch the sheriff to the livery, when Hank noticed Deputy Peabody up the street. Clifton reluctantly put the muzzle of his six-gun in his step-brother's ribs, while Hank started up the street for the deputy.

Getwood was desperate. At first he pleaded with his brother to let him go and he wouldn't bother the family or the ranch, but he would track down his dad's killers and bring them to justice. Clifton was just not in any mood to yield to Getwood's wishes, at least until after he and Hank both talked to the sheriff.

Ranger was trying to follow Hank, who was on his way up the snowy street to confront the Deputy Peabody.

The old dog was having a tough time maneuvering because of the depth of the snow, so he would jump from one spot to another, while trying to keep up with the cowboy. The sun was burning it's name in the snow and some of the ground was turning into mud holes, as the mystifying weather prevailed.

Hiram McCoy made the mistake of walking in the aisle to fetch a grain bucket to start the morning feeding for the horses.

Getwood suddenly reached forward and grabbed Hiram by his arm, spun his back around, and placed a head-lock around his neck. At the same time he lifted the gun from Hiram's holster and put it tight against the head of the frightened stable man.

"Get outta my way, Clifton, and you drop your gun, If you don't want to see ol' man McCoy's brains on the floor of this coop he calls a stable." Getwood was adamant, and as deliberate as a house cat with it's mind made up

"If you holler out, brother, I'll shoot this ol' man fer sure. All right," he said to the struggling attendant, "get my saddle on that crop-eared horse, and be quick. Do it now!"

Clifton dropped his weapon and stared in amazement as his brother went with this act.

Cliff didn't attempt to interfere, with respect for Hiram, but he began to question Getwood's reasoning.

"What's Momma gonna think, Get? Don't you suppose with what's happened with Dad, and now what you're doing, that she may not be able to deal with this situation?"

""I can't help it. Ever'one's agin me, and I ain't got time to explain anythin' now. You'll jist have to tell her I'm sorry about Pap, but I had nary a thang to do with it. I-I'll write her a letter, okay? McCoy you got the horse tacked, now you best jist ease back outta my way, and stand over by Clifton. I'm a-leavin' and nobody better come after me. I've got his gun and the rifle that's on my saddle."

Getwood rode out the back way and into the drifted snow that was starting to melt.

Hank knew nothing of what was taking place simultaneously at the livery stable. He was just catching up to the deputy in the fast thaw of the sloppy street, and asking to accompany him to the sheriff's office.

"Howdy, Hank Hall," said Deputy Peabody, "That'us some snowfall we had, sure 'nuf. I'm on my way to the Palace fer some breakfast, you a-comin', too?"

Hank said, "Never mind, Peabody, if Sheriff Sager's in his office, I'd as soon see him."

"Yeah, he's there, all right. He et a'ready."

Hank finally got to the board planking in front of the sheriff's office, where the jail was, and stomped the mud and snow from his boots before going inside. Ranger shook himself, but he waited until he was inside the office, first.

"G'mornin', Jim. I've not got time for all the story this minute, but you had best come with me to the livery. There's a mess, and my cousin, Getwood, is involved. Clifton is there, watching him and waiting for you. Uh, Jim," Hank continued, in a dire and very serious tone of voice, "Clyde Hall is dead."

"Dead? . . . . Clyde? Well, wha . . ."

"Shot in the back, Jim. Cliff and I found him last evening and brought him into town. It started to snow on us about halfway here. His body is over to the livery stable."

"What happened?" The sheriff wanted to know. He put on his canvas-covered, wool-lined outer-coat, as he bolted out the door with Hank and the dog following.

"I'm sure it has to do with all the cattle rustling that's been going on, Jim. Somehow, I-we think that Getwood's mighty involved."

"You mean you and Clifton? You boys got any proof? Is this part of this Farris feller killing? I've not heard back from Carson City on that yet."

Hank explained about letting Clyde ride his bay horse, Lawyer, and the horse returning without Clyde. He told how he and Clifton found the body at the mesa road to their Blue Sands pasture, on the way to where he and Cliff moved some of their yearlings.

"I figure the one who shot my uncle must've mistook him for me. It could've been from cover on the mesa, and he recognized my bay horse, and automatically figured I was a-ridin' him."

"That's good figurin', son. How's Lucille takin' this? Does she know how you and Cliff feel about her other boy?" The sheriff kept questioning Hank as they approached the livery.

"What have you done with Getwood?" he said. "What's he doin' here?"

The sheriff and Hank walked in the barn and saw Cliff and Hiram, who was still feeding the sorrel team the Hall's drove in.

"Where's Getwood?" Hank asked Clifton.

* * *

Ren and Lefty were making their way, wearily, to the pasture Getwood described as holding the Circle Diamond yearling cattle. It had stopped snowing since the two left the confines of the livery and the wrath of Getwood, but the fast melting snow presented some very unusual problems.

"Whut'r you stoppin' fer, Lefty?" Ren asked, as they rode along together.

"It's my dag-gum ol' horse. He's ballin'-up pretty bad, and I got to clean all of his feet."

As the snow started to melt, it became more workable as a matter that was easy to pack when pressed. The horse picked up mud balls mixed together with snow in its hooves as it traveled along.

It wasn't just Lefty's pinto, it was happening to Ren's roan pony, too. Both men dismounted to clean their animal's feet.

"I don't feel worth a damn. My head hurts ever when I bend over, like this."

"Yer own damn fault," Ren said, to his complaining cohort. "You never could hold any liquor. Mazie says you always throw-up in her room, and smell-up everything."

"Izzat so?" Lefty countered. "I s'pose you are able to last the night without that problem? I notice you git to whars you lose track o'them card hands in the Monte and poker games, and lose all yer dough. You know," Lefty continued, "you're into me now fer . . .let's see, uh, forty six dollars."

"Forty-two," answered Ren, as he leaned over and vomited in the melting snow.

* * *

THE BROTHERS-IN LAW FIND THE HERD

Clifton was attempting to answer Hank's question about Getwood's disappearance, when the sheriff arrived at the stable.

"Aw, Hank," Cliff said, "he's gone! Lit out the back way a few minutes ago, whilst you was fetchin' Sheriff Sager."

"What do you suppose is going on here, this morning?" The sheriff wanted to know.

"My step-brother sort of got the drop on us, and took Hiram's pistol. Made him saddle ol' Croppy, and rode out in a hurry. I couldn't just shoot him, I-I mean might have hit Hiram. H-he threatened to shoot Hiram if I interfered. He held the pistol up to his head."

They tried to explain it all to Sheriff Sager, and in the meantime, Getwood was gaining distance with his getaway.

"This is Uncle Clyde's body, Jim," Hank said, when he pointed to the wrapped, tarpaulin-covered corpse resting on several bales of hay.

"Clifton, I surely am sorry to hear about ol' Clyde. I reckon he was 'bout the best friend I've had since I took this law job. Does your mother know? Is she going to be all right? I hardly know just what to say."

The sheriff was visibly wrought, yet he knew there was more that he hadn't been told.

"Just what was Getwood's role in all this?" He sat down on a hay bale next to Clyde's body, and said to Hiram, "Why'nt you go fetch Caleb, and have him take Clyde's body to his funeral parlor? I think you'll want Preacher Dalton to know, Cliff, as soon as you can, Then, we'll think about what to do about Getwood."

"I figure we ought to saddle up and go after Getwood as soon as we can," Hank was speaking to Clifton and the sheriff. "The snow's melting and the tracking will be at its best. Besides, he may just lead us to where we can catch any others that could be involved."

"Hiram, before you fetch Caleb, will you put ol' Ranger in that empty box-stall, 'til we come back for the team? We should be back soon, and he'll be all right in there."

Cliff drifted over to the other side of the aisle where other horses were all standing hip-shot in their tie-stalls, and admired a big, white-footed sorrel with a flaxen mane and tail.

"All right if I use this one, Hiram? He has the conformation of a good runner."

"Boys, I'll get Peabody and Martin and Soapy McClure, and catch my horse. We can have a big posse pretty quick. I can swear you boys in with the rest when we meet back here in - say, about twenty minutes," the sheriff hollered over his shoulder, as he hustled up the muddy street.

"I'm ridin' across and over to the preacher's house," Hank mentioned to Cliff, "while you're saddlin' your horse. I know he'll make all the arrangements that need be. It sure will help us when it comes time to fetch Abbey and Aunt Lucy for the buryin' ceremony. I'll be back 'fore the sheriff and the rest will."

Clifton had to finally help Hiram catch ol' Ranger and put him in the empty box-stall. He was lying next to his master's body and didn't want to leave him. Hiram closed the stall door, but forgot to shut the back window.

Lefty Barker and Ren Morgan managed to sober themselves enough to remount after tending to their horse's feet, and started their journey toward the Blue Sand mountain pasture that held the Circle Diamond beeves.

"Jeezus, Ren, I'm s-so damn cold, I feel like I'm a-gonna freeze to death." Lefty was continually complaining to Ren.

"Shut-up," Ren snorted his answer. "I'm tired of hearin' you complain'n all the time. We get these steers out of here and over to Miller Canyon with the rest, and git 'em branded and loaded tomorrow night, we'll be good."

Think of what all that money we're a-gonna split kin buy you. Probably enough of them long-johns' and extry blankets to keep you warm all winter long."

"Looky there," Lefty cried, as he pulled his coat collar away from in front of his face. "From this rise we're on, I kin see the big warter-tank. That snow's startin' to melt, and them bovines will be comin' over to warter pretty soon."

"All's we gots to do is build us a trap on thet lee side. They's 'nuf brush on the back side to hold 'em all in."

The two, sorry, brother's-in-law started to drag some logs and brush to surround one side of the represso, where the water was, and hide themselves back among the trees. When the cattle came to water, they would let them drink their fill, then bunch them and drive the gather toward the opening into Miller Canyon.

Ren stepped off his roan horse to start a small fire, and proceeded to unpack a quart of whiskey from his saddle bag.

"Here's to good fortune," he said, and took the first huge swallow.

CHAPTER ELEVEN

A NEW GANG IS FORMED

The abandoned shack on the Dixon property was nearly covered by the drifted snow. It was built under a promontory that once abutted a large body of water that formed there eons before, and since dried up. It was normally accessible, yet very well hidden.

The snow that blew against it was starting to melt, as Getwood urged his crop-eared horse just a little closer.

Thin wisps of blue-gray smoke funneled its way upward from the cabin, until it dissipated with the wind. Getwood pulled rein on ol' Croppy, and proceeded to step off and try to hide himself among the tree line. He warily sought a closer look at the cabin that he now knew was occupied.

While scanning the bare scene, he saw two saddle horses in the nearby corral, Those horses suddenly got wind of Getwood and nickered enough that Croppy answered before Get could reach up with his hand to muzzle him.

The stillness afforded by the light blanket of snow allowed any sound to be amplified, thus granting those inside to acknowledge the noise their horses made.

"Who's out there?" came one voice from inside. This was followed by a sharp rifle report that caused his horse, as well as Get, to react.

It was apparent to Getwood the individuals in the cabin were not Ren or Lefty. He wondered who would be using this place that very few knew of. His plan was to tie his horse at the edge of the tree line, so it could be seen from the cabin, while he would climb around the back side and jump down to the roof.

He had Hiram's hand gun in his belt, and took the rifle with him. There was only one door and only one window in this crude structure, but the heavy logs it was built with were chinked well. This kept the heat in and the weather out.

It wasn't easy for Getwood to climb the rangy fir tree at the back side that led to the promontory. He fell the first try and ripped his coat. When he finally succeeded in reaching the snow-covered overhang, he carefully half-slid and half-dropped to the cabin roof, about ten feet beneath the overhang.

Next, he removed his torn coat and used a part of the sleeve to stuff into the chimney extension pipe to choke back the smoke from the fireplace below. He also packed snow on top of it to make certain it worked.

* * *

The Walker-Mills Mining Company was robbed of its payroll during the night. Two employees, Frank Palmer and Myles Cooke, were the perpetrators, who, by accident, discovered this abandoned cabin. Within five minutes the small room was filling with wood smoke. The furious miners had no choice but to run outside.

Falling out the door first was Frank Palmer, who had his bandanna held to his face, stifling and gagging. Myles Cooke was right behind, and even with his gun in hand, had no way to even see his target, let alone be able to shoot at it.

"All right, you two, no tricks. Toss your guns by that big rock over there, and walk toward the corral," Get shouted instructions, as he attempted to jump down from the front of the roof to the ground by the front door. He had already taken the plug from the chimney pipe, and he threw his smudged coat down first.

"That's far enough, you boys jes squat right where you are." Getwood walked to where his horse was tied and brought him by the cabin. He took his rope from the saddle and placed the big loop over both men, whom he instructed to stand-up, back to back.

He pulled them both to one of the nearby trees and wound the rope around them and then around the tree. Getwood then unsaddled his horse and put him in the corral with the others,

Get picked up the guns by the rock and he looked inside the cabin. Most of the smoke was cleared by now, so he decided to enter. To his ultimate surprise, there, on the table, in two neatly stacked piles, was more money than he'd ever seen. The valise on the floor held more.

* * *

"You kin have the last swaller of this," Ren told Lefty. "See'n as you're always so blame cold all'a time."

Lefty was already so drunk that he dropped the bottle when Ren passed it to him.

"Damn you, boy!" Ren slurred.

Lefty tried three times before he could get his foot in the stirrup, to mount.

"Them steers'll be comin' to warter soon and you cain't even see."

"I-I kin too, see!" Lefty replied, as he shook down a loop with his catch rope. He spurred his horse and whooped a holler, as he looked back at Ren.

"N-not yet, ya gotta has pa-paashens." Within several minutes the first two of the yearlings made an appearance at the watering place. "S-sh-sh," Ren burped, to his drunken partner, "Don't lettum schee-us."

It was nothing but dumb luck and some gross stupidity on the part of the cattle, that the two men were able to split and gather at least twelve steers. The balance of the yearlings raced past the unguarded opening in the brushy confines, and escaped to bunch themselves about a quarter of a mile away.

Lefty fell off his Pinto, twice during this procedure, and twice was able to remount and continue. He moved the steers to the spot where they'd earlier cut the fence.

Both men were adept at the cowboy trade, but they were fortunate their mistakes were not of consequence, as they moved their prizes toward Miller Canyon.

* * *

Word travels quickly in small towns, and when Mary Anne learned of Clyde Hall's death, she decided to hire a horse and buggy and make the fourteen mile trip out to the Circle Diamond.

When Mary Anne arrived at the livery stable, she saw the sorrel team of Circle Diamond horses and asked Hiram to explain. He told her of the shenanigans Getwood pulled, and warned her that as far as he knew, "Missus Lucille warn't awares that there was a posse out after her boy, Getwood."

Mary Anne was certain that Abbey was in just as much wonderment about Hank, and when she got to the cow ranch, she and Abbey would be able to discuss the situation and offer solace to Hank's Aunt Lucy.

Hiram McCoy harnessed a fine black mare he called Jamima, for Mary Anne to use. The mare was a deep-chested Morgan that was well broken to harness, and a willing equine with no quit in her. Mary Anne tapped her once with the reins, then pulled the blanket around her knees and waist and started out.

It was nearing mid-day and the sun was somewhat warming the temperature and slowly melting the remaining snow. The wind that was blowing from the north-west was sure to gather in some more bad weather, but for now, the clouds were high. Mary Anne was concerned that Getwood may double back to the ranch and she feared that perhaps Abbey may be in some unforeseen danger.

* * *

"I know I've seen that feller somewhere." The two crooks were trying to loosen themselves from the tree, as Myles Cooke repeated himself. "I got it! I met that guy in the pen in Carson City, years ago. He helped another feller an me to 'scape."

"He had a few 'friends' on the inside, but someone blew the whistle on him'n he never ratted on us. Uh . . .lessee . . . Boyle! That's it. That's his name. It's him, Frank. He'll let us go when I tell him who I am, I think it . . ."

"You sure 'bout this, Cookie? You think he'll remember you?"

"Hey, Boyle," Myles hollered to Getwood. "C'mere, onest. Hit's me, 'Cookie', from the big house in Carson. Remember me, Boyle?, Myles Cooke. You helped me big time. C'mere, let us go and we'll cut you . . ."

"Hold on, Cookie, we ain't cuttin' him in on our deals," Frank said, positively.

Getwood suddenly appeared in front of the two, and laughed at the recognition.

"Cooke the crook," he said. "I remember, I always wondered what happened to you. Wher'n hell did you get all that money?" "It come from the mine office, and the bank in Tonopah? Whatter you a-doin' here?"

Get untied the pair and still held a drop on them as he said, "Long story. There's a Canyon about a half days ride from here, where some of my pals have a jerk of young heifers and steers holed up. I'm hopin' they're on their way to pick up at least another dozen or so more if the Circle Diamond ranch yearlings. We got a rail car due at the Blackwood siding tomorrow night, and these yearlin's'll give us a full load." Get was explaining this all to Palmer and Cooke as they entered into the secluded cabin.

"Rustlin', huh? That sounds good to us," Cooke said to Getwood. "Frank, I think we ought to cut ol' Boyle, here, a part of our swag, in turn for us sharing his little rustlin' scheme."

Palmer wasn't sold on the idea, but he had no choice as long as Get held a gun on them.

"Well, you lay that gun down, friend, and I 'spect I'll go along with the deal. How many men are in with you, and whatta ya think they'll say to our deal?"

"We don't mention the bank caper, or any other money. There's two of 'em, but they're dumber'n a box of rocks."

Palmer still wasn't completely sold on the outcome of the venture, and looked at Myles with a quizzical expression.

"Sounds okay to me," Myles finally said, reassuring Palmer. Don't worry about it, let Boyle handle it with them other men."

Getwood further explained they'd be able to split some rustling gains without much trouble.

"There's a lot more cattle here that are gonna soon need a new home."

Getwood thought he made all this pretty clear, and as he finished talking, the three shook hands and counted all the money on the table.

Cooke emptied the valise on the floor, and they all started stacking the bills.

CHAPTER TWELVE

STOLEN STEERS AND A HORSE TRADE

The posse had been gone only for a few minutes when Ranger managed to run from one side of the stall wall and leap through the open window. When he landed he was met by Hiram's dog, Molly, who was in season and looking at a quick romance. Ranger was torn from his thoughts of pursuing Hank and Cliff, to just answer the call of the wild as it presented itself. He chose the latter, and thus he delayed his journey for a short while.

After a brief respite, he bade a farewell to his companion and started again on his course.

The trail ol' Ranger followed was easier for it was tromped down by the six horses ridden by the lawmen and their sworn-in deputies.

Clifton was calling to Hank while they rode side by side. "This snow's melting so fast that we'll have to look carefully for ol' Croppy's tracks. There's plenty of other tracks showin' up. I think he's headin' for the Blue Sands, anyway, so let's head for thar direction," Cliff announced .

"Why don't we just ask ol' Ranger?"

"Ranger!!" Clifton gasped. He turned in his saddle to see their good ranch dog bounding after the group, tongue out, and yelping as he closed in to them.

"Hiram must'a let him out. He's a determined rascal, ain't he, boys?" Hank was still chuckling when he whistled at the dog. "Look here, boys! He said to the posse. "These are Croppy's tracks, and they seem to lead north toward the old Dixon property."

* * *

"What's your plan about them steers your men are to hold with some of the others?" Palmer asked. Getwood said then, he figured the boys would brand any slicks, and change brands on the ones that needed it. He told him it would be done with running irons and they could alter a mark to match those papers he had for the stock-yard inspector.

"That inspector in Carson City is workin' with my man, Lefty, so we won't hav. . ."

"Lefty? Lefty Barker? Cookie yelled to Get.

"Sure is, how'd you come to know him?"

"Hell, he's one of the guys from the pen in Carson, ain't he? I remember it all now. You two knew each other then, too. Am I right?" Myles was smiling at Frank, when he asked Getwood the questions.

"You know that stock yard inspector was my contact when I make my escape. I know Lefty Barker was a kin to him, and he helped me by contacting that guy to git me a job in the stock yards. Whooee, we lucked out, sure!"

"Well," Getwood said, "these beeves that were a-gittin' are comin' from the Circle Diamond, and that's my ranch. Matter of fact, the folks there adopted me as their son, years ago. My so-called brother is tryin' to take over the place, now that my Dad has been killed. My cousin, Hank Hall, is the one that is a thorn in my side."

"He suspects me of rustlin', but he can't prove it. Worse matter is, Lefty thought that he shot and killed that damn Hank Hall, but my Dad was ridin' Hall's bay horse that evenin', and that dumb Lefty Barker shot my Dad, instead."

* * *

Miller Canyon was somewhat of an enigma, in that the snow that fell earlier, drifted to the far southeast side. It lay mostly against the tall, side-stone walls that formed a very large circle. This arc girded most of the territory and lofted very high on the north side of these Canyon walls.

Plenty of water and good grass prevailed, and the gather of cattle already placed there, were in very good condition.

Ren and Lefty were successfully driving the steers into the throat of the Canyon, toward the first of the large water holes, inside. The crude corral they built weeks ago was still in good repair for them to utilize with this gather of cow animals.

None of this bunch had been branded, but they were quickly penned, a fire built and running irons heated, for the upcoming task.

Ren's roan horse was a stout animal, and although tired from the drive, was eager to please his rider who would rope the first steer by both small horns.

Lefty was sober enough by now to complete the job. He snaked his loop into the path of the rear legs of the bovine, and caught them both. He pitched his slack and then turned his pinto away from the catch to stretch out the rope.

This move straightened out and flattened the steer. The roping horses were well trained and both faced their quarry, while keeping the ropes taut. The men scampered to tie the feet so the steer could be branded.

This job took them more than two full hours to catch and brand all the beeves. The horses and the men were both exhausted.

* * *

"Well, let me get this straight," Cookie said. "The yearlin's that Lefty and the other feller are after are all from your ranch?"

"My folks started that ranch, along with my Dad's brother and his wife, who are both dead now. I call 'em my folks 'cause they kinda raised me over time. My Dad's brother and wife had a son, and that's this here, Hank Hall, I'm a-tellin' you about. Him and his wife are livin' at the ranch, too."

"See, my folks had a son afore they adopted me; he's a foster brother, I reckon." Getwood explained all this very carefully, and finished by telling them that everyone in this territory knows him as "Getwood Hall." He also told them that his prison records list his name as "Franklin Boyle."

"Only you and Lefty, and now you, Frank, know me by the name of Boyle. The shipping papers I got for the stockyards people has my name as Thomas Woods. Don't fergit that. I don't care nuthin' fer anyone else, 'ceptin' maybe my Ma, Lucille Hall. She's been right good to me. It ain't like she ain't bein' took care of. They's plenty folks as neighbors to watch out fer her. . . I got no regrets . . .understand?"

The two outlaws listened to Getwood and they seemed to understand, but being outside the law, they had to rely on their own wits to survive. They both took the mine jobs with the sole purpose of eventually robbing the payroll. It took time, but they finally did it. Now, they decided that cattle rustling was less risky and a whole lot easier.

The wind was as sharp as a fine honed razor when it whistled over the open expanse of land where the posse was debating a trail to the Dixon property. The sheriff ordered his men to follow him out in the direction toward that property, as Hank rode up to ask him a few questions.

"What do you surmise to do with Get, Jim, when we find him? We have never caught him actually doin' any rustling."

"I 'spect we can bring him into town and question him about the characters you've seen him with, and I intend to find out all about his messin' up Hiram and Clifton at the livery stable this mornin'. I'm not at all too happy with this chasin' and ridin', even if it is a part of my job," he said, smiling.

A lone rider on a bald-faced, sorrel horse was heading on a course due west of the posse, and Martin Reyes, one of the deputized men, suddenly spotted him and alerted the rest of the posse members.

"*Aqüi, Hombrés, a la derécha. Una moménto*" The posse turned at Reyes request and started to surround the rider.

"Howdy, Cliff, Hank. H'lo, Jim. What is all the fuss about? the rider wanted to know, while he reined in his nice, big sorrel.

"Glad to see it's you, Harry. What are you doin' on this range?" Sheriff Sager awaited his answer.

"Oh, it's Harry Carter," Hank said to Clifton. "Are you still having all those rustler problems, Harry?"

"Not since I lost them five beeves last month. I'm riding this west pasture checking the fence lines. The storm may have laid some posts down, and I intend to run some stock here pretty soon."

"What are you doing here, anyway? Is this some sort of a posse?" Harry asked.

"Yes, it is," the sheriff replied. "You may as well let me swear you in, too, and join us. We're all a-lookin' for Getwood Hall. Cliff will fill you in as we ride on. C'mon, Harry, raise your hand."

"I'm powerful sorry about Caroline, Cliff. How're you holdin' up?" Harry asked.

"It's been mighty rough, Harry, then we just found Daddy, shot and killed, and Hank and I figure Getwood's involved in this mess, too."

"W-what? You sayin' your dad's dead, Cliff? My lord, I never knew nothin' abo . . ."

"How would you know, Harry? It just happened." Cliff explained the horrid details.

Hank rode up alongside the pair and asked Harry how his wife was doing. "Is she about ready to have that baby, yet?" Cliff leaned across his saddle to hear an answer.

"Hey, boys, I'm already a father. Fern had two fine babies, all at once, three days ago."

"They call them twins, Harry. But we never knew nothin' about you folks havin' babies . . ."

"Well, how would either of you know?" Harry was laughing when he said, "It just happened."

* * *

"That's a fine lookin' dapple-gray horse you have, Cookie," said Getwood, as they all reached the corral. "If you're a gambling' man, I'll just make you a deal for my sorrel horse."

"I know that crop-eared sucker that you're a ridin' is a good'un. He's big and stout, and could pack a feller my size all day. What's on your mind?"

"I'll play you three hands of show-down," Get answered. "We'll let Frank cut and I'll deal. Best two out of three hands wins the others horse. Whatta ya say?"

Cookie laughed. "Frank can cut and deal."

Getwood nodded and held two fingers behind Cookie's back for Frank to see, but Palmer wasn't as dumb as he let on. He interpreted the signal to mean there would be two extra beeves for him to split, if he 'worked' the cards in Get-woods favor.

Palmer promptly saw to it with the first hand. Getwood had two Kings and Cookie had a pair of threes. The second hand was the last. Cooke was dealt a pair of Queens. Getwood won with three fives.

"What am I gonna ride?" Cookie asked.

"Hey, sport," Getwood mused, "for a hundred dollars you can but Croppy." Away they rode, joking, toward Miller Canyon.

CHAPTER THIRTEEN

AN OLD FRIEND IS GONE . . . FOREVER

The tracks of the Circle Diamond horse that Getwood was riding became more recognizable as Hank followed Croppy's hoof-prints into the tree line that bordered the outskirts of the Dixon property's log cabin.

"I don't see anything from here, Sheriff," he said, as he slid down from the young gelding he was on and tied him to a small tree. "It looks like some tracks over there. In fact, those are Croppy's tracks. He was tied up here, and . . ."

"Looks like the rider went to the cabin," said Clifton, "and left his horse here. Hold on, he came came back and led him toward the corral, over yonder."

"There's been more then one person here," the sheriff hollered to the group. "There were at least two other horses in the corral, and thet cabin smells like the fireplace backed-up on 'em.

"It's plumb full of stale smoke." "Hey, there's still a pot of beans in here, sittin' on the stove," said Soapy. Peabody was assuring the rest, also, by shouting his decision.

Hank and Cliff, and Harry Carter were near the corral when they all discovered in which direction a group of three horse and riders rode away, including ol' Croppy.

"This here trail leads to Miller Canyon," Harry told the posse.

"We'll foller it, boys, er- won't we, Sheriff?"

Deputy Peabody was standing in his stirrups when he spoke, and realized he was not in charge of this brigade.

"Reckon we will," Jim Sager replied. "Keep an eye on those Circle Diamond horse tracks, Hank, and they'll lead us to the man we want."

"Good thing we got us seven riders," Peabody said, "them fellers is three, now."

Sue enough, as the afternoon wore on, the high clouds were dropping and the sharp wind was now starting to cut into the groups faces. It was getting colder with each step the tired, posse horses took.

Harry Carter was well prepared for bad weather with his two pair of long-johns and a scarf tied around his felt hat and under his chin. These Nevada buckaroos were well aware that this high country weather could easily change without a moments notice, and usually carried an extra coat and wore their legging chaps.

"There's a good chance that we'll find these crooks at Miller Canyon, although I'm not real sure just why they'd tail it to there," Sheriff Sager announced to the tired group.

* * *

Getwood, who was proudly mounted on the good, gray horse that once was Cooke's, pulled up for a minute on the trail. He was digging in his chaps for an old stub of a pencil, and looking in his saddle bag for a scrap of paper from his tally-book.

"Since I've got to get to Carson City afore this week's done, I'm leavin' you boys with a note to Lefty and Ren from me. It'll explain everything, and tell 'em you both are workin' with me in all this."

"You're gonna find 'em at Miller Canyon, and you can help 'em move the cattle to the train siding, and help 'em load the critters. They know I'm to meet them at the old cabin where I found you, so, jes hole-up there, 'til I return."

"You bring that cattle money with you, Boyle, and we'll merge it with our mine company payroll. We can be decidin' on our next move whilst we're a-waitin' fer you," Cookie explained.

"Hey, where you headin' now, a-goin' off in that direction?" Frank Palmer questioned Get. "That's not the way to Carson City."

"I know it ain't, I'm gonna swing back past the home ranch one more time. I've got to pick up my possibles, take care of something personal, and then head for Carson City."

Getwood turned off the old trail to Miller Canyon, while Myles Cooke and Frank Palmer headed on to meet with Ren and Lefty.

Freezing rain followed the trail leading from Miller Canyon, and traveled on south-west toward the cow ranch, and home.

"Ol' Blue," Getwood said to his newly acquired dapple-gray gelding, "you sure are a fine animal. You cost me the profit off'n two beeves to Palmer, but I got paid plenty for that sorrel," he laughed.

The wind blew harder the moment Get left the partial wind-break of the back side of the Blue Sand mountains. It drove the icy rain against the side of the horse and the rider, and caused Getwood to buckle his slicker tighter around his scrawny neck.

His hat was dripping rain water from the front depression like a waterfall cascading down a mountain side.

* * *

A nice fire was warming the folks in the main house at the Circle Diamond ranch. Aunt Lucy just finished tucking Clifton's baby boy into his bedroom crib, and was returning to her rocking chair beside the crackling fireside.

Mary Anne said she would help Abbey start a fire to warm her cabin, in case Hank would ride in yet tonight, but she would sleep on the couch in the parlor. Aunt Lucy just wouldn't hear of it.

"Nonsense, Mary Ann. You are going to sleep in the other bedroom." she stated emphatically. The young women bundled up well before going over to Abbey's cabin. The icy rain was turning to snow again, as Getwood rode the gray gelding into the ranch barn.

* * *

It as getting late and most of the daylight was used up for the posse that was on the trail of three horses and the riders heading toward Miller Canyon.

"Hold up, boys!" Sheriff Sager stepped off his horse and proceeded to don his slicker that was tied to his saddle cantle.

"It's getting dark and we're going to lose the tracks, besides, I never did intend for us to be gone this long. We'll head back for Walker Lake and decide about coming back tomorrow."

"Let me have Deputy Peabody, Jim," Cliff said to the sheriff. "That's my brother among two others, heading for the Canyon. Peabody and I can shelter-up in those rock caves tonight, and keep an eye on 'em, 'til you get back here,"

The sheriff decided that was a good idea. He could bring out some food and a few more men. "Harry, I know you should be t'home with your wife and new babies, and Soapy and Marty, you boys'll be able to get a fresh start tomorrow. What's on your mind, Hank?"

"Well, that's fine with me if Pea and Cliff will stay here. I think I'll try to follow these tracks that cut from the rest, for as long as I can. They seem to be headed for the direction of our ranch, but belong to a different horse, a larger one with bigger hoofs."

Now it was only two tracks leading into Miller Canyon, and one of them belonged to the crop-eared, sorrel horse.

Hank whistled for Ranger and the two started toward the home ranch. It was clear one of the tracks belonged to a horse they'd all tracked from the Dixon property, over toward Miller Canyon. Hank wondered why, at the entrance to the pass, this track cut off from the others, and led the way it did.

Ol' Ranger was making it pretty well with the exception that ever so often, he'd whimper when the ice caked in his toes, and he'd have to stop and chew at the ice balls in his feet.

The young sorrel horse that Hank rode was holding up better than Hank thought he would. He was four and close to five years old, and a horses' back has developed to maturity by then.

Hank never saw the big badger that attacked his dog with such ferocity that they rolled over and over. Ranger was trying to escape the snarling, vise-clamp jaws of the more stout, meaner and quicker beast.

Hank had never fired a weapon off the back of this young sorrel, so he quickly stepped down and fired at the badger from a few yards.

It was a direct hit that killed the feral animal, but Hank left the badger, as he raced to the side of the faithful dog, who, bleeding profusely, lay dying along the cold, mucky trail.

Hank tenderly cradled his pal, who looked hauntingly in his eyes as if to say, "We're parting, but I'll understand."

At the risk of losing precious light that may help him continue to follow the horse tracks, Hank buried ol' Ranger's body on a small hillside that overlooked the big Nevada range the dog so loved. He vowed to return someday and place a marker on the grave with Ranger's name on it.

First, he had to take care of business. The slicker he wore helped keep him dry, but the relentless, sleeting, freezing rain was a worrisome pestilence that made him long to be warm and dry, and deep in his darling Abbey's loving arms.

Hank strained to make out the tracks he'd been following, but somehow, even with the delay and the terrible accident with

Ranger, the one track he could follow lead directly to the Circle Diamond ranch.

He liked the way the horse responded. He did only a minimum of shying, and that was unusual for a 'teen-aged' horse so full of himself. He thought some more about this horse, and decided it was time to name him.

He mulled over several names before he decided on the name of 'Rainy Day Rascal'. He'd call him 'Rainy'.

Soapy McClure, Marty Reyés and Sheriff Sager arrived in a street darkened Walker Lake a little before midnight. They agreed to meet at the stable in the morning and continue plans.

Clifton and Deputy Peabody sought solace in one of the ledge-caves near the entrance to Miller Canyon. They started a cook fire and roasted two errant jack-rabbits that wandered too close. At least they were dry and fed, and would take turns watching the Canyon entrance.

Harry Carter was on his way home with a sudden urge to see Fern and hold his twin babies and he was as cold as a marked deck of cards, as he had to face the severe, extreme weather while he headed west.

* * *

Cooke and Palmer rode through the Canyon entrance late afternoon, as the wind driven rain commenced to drizzle. They spotted the corral and the fenced pasture, where cattle were grazing. Near the corral was a tarpaulin pitched in a way to effect a temporary shelter. Several extremely large, gray boulders stood behind the brush-covered area where the makeshift tent was set-up. A cook fire was serving as warmth as well as stoking a large pot of strong coffee.

The aroma was increasing when the two robbers approached.

CHAPTER FOURTEEN

A NEFARIOUS COWARD
AND A DISCOVERY

A single lantern dimly lit the cozy bedroom where Abbey and Hank stayed in their cabin on the Circle Diamond cow ranch.

"I really miss you, my love," she sighed to herself while she spoke aloud. It could be possible, she thought, that her handsome cowboy would ride in, yet tonight. She brought some of the left-over stew Aunt Lucy fixed for supper, and she kept it warm for Hank on the hearth.

The cold rain was aggravating more lightning by now. Getwood was glad to reach the barn at the cow ranch and put ol' Blue in a dry stall. He noted there was no light in the main ranch house, but he was certain he saw one in Hank and Abbey's cabin.

Getwood slipped from the barn to the un-occupied bunkhouse where he stayed when he was on the ranch. He closed the shutters on the front window before he lit the lantern inside.

It was time to make a decision that could change his life. He knew he wasn't to be included in the operation of the Circle

Diamond, and he decided that living outside the law would allow him a freedom he wanted, and also garner him a lot of money.

Getwood carefully selected most of his items to pack in his 'war-bag' that he'd take along on the sixty-two mile ride to the stock yards in Carson City. After he packed all his 'possibles', he doused the lantern and headed for the barn.

He liked the dapple-gray horse he got from Cooke, and since he'd ridden him earlier, decided to use him as a pack horse and place his saddle on Jiggs.

It as apparent to Getwood that he take some food and water with him. He readied the horses and passed through the barn where he noticed an unhitched buggy, staves down, sitting in the aisle. In one of the box stalls stood a black mare that he knew belonged to the town livery. Someone was visiting. Who could it be, he thought, while he silently made his way to the ranch house kitchen.

Getwood had to pass the cabin where Abbey was, and noticed the chimney smoke and a muffled light from the semi-closed shutter, in an otherwise jet-black, rain-filled night.

He paused at the half-open window where he could see through the wind-blown curtains, into the room where Abbey was.

Mary Anne was awakened by a shake of thunder that followed a close-by lightning flash. She sat up in bed and peered outside her window that faced the back room of the cabin. It was only for an instant, but she was sure she saw someone trying to get in.

Mary Anne quickly dressed, and determined not to awaken Aunt Lucy or the baby, fumbled in the room's darkness for the lantern and a safety match. She made it to the kitchen table where she immediately lit the lantern and began searching for the butcher knife. In her haste she neglected to put on an outer coat, but started out the door toward Abbey's cabin.

* * *

"You snake!," she cried, "you no-good bastard, take your filthy, smelly, hands off . . ."

"Shut up, you slut. Your fancy cowboy ain't anywhere around, an' I intend to make you fergit all 'bout him, anyways." Getwood ripped Abbey's nightgown when he lurched at her when he leapt inside her window. She threw the half-filled basin from the night stand at his leering, rain-soaked body. This only diverted his left hand from her exposed bosom. He proceeded to slam his fist into Abbey's face, and knocked her into the dresser beside the bed.

"It ain't no use to scream out, you whore, with this storm they's no one gonna' hear you." Getwood slapped her once more across her mouth, and this time, drew blood when he threw her on the bed comforter. He then savagely tore away Abbey's remaining clothes and attempted to unfasten his britches.

"You miserable wretch, you know Hank will kill you for this. Let me go - now," she cried.

* * *

The front door of the cabin was not bolted. Mary Anne called out Abbey's name when she entered the warm, dry room. The fire place reflected a yellow-red glow that brightened the room from the night's darkness.

"Abbey!" Mary Anne called, again. "What is it? Are you all right? Let me in . . . Abbey-"

In seconds from when Getwood heard someone call from the front room, he gathered himself and crawled back outside through the window, cursing his luck. He raced to the barn stopping only for water at the trough.

Out through the back corral gate he fled. The dapple-gray horse was loaded with his worldly goods, and he whipped Jiggs out of pure frustration, from having been thwarted from his lust and revenge.

He was hoping to finish what he'd started with Abbey, and get even with Hank for everything he hated in him. He couldn't admit to jealously, but he felt now, he would get even for what

Cliff and Hank, and even his father, had said to him over the years. Getwood was well on his way to Carson City, and the heavier rain would certainly wash out his tracks.

* * *

"Hey, Peabody," Clifton spoke softly to the deputy. The dawn greeted the pair with considerable crispness, but was warming steadily now that the rain was finished.

"Look over toward that stand of tall trees -more to your right. Isn't that a corral down there, next to those boulders?"

"Yup, I believe it is, Cliff. You think that's where the men rode to last night?"

Clifton quickly doused the small fire he'd built back in the cave, afraid that the smoke might be spotted. "Sure wish we had some coffee to start this day," Pea remarked.

"Wal, Cliff, I figure Jim's leavin' town 'bout now, and him and the men he's bringin' ought to be here in a hour or so."

"Quick, Peabody, look to the corral. I seen a bunch of cattle moving around there, See?"

"You're right, Cliff, 'cept I don't see them two fellers we was a-follerin' last evening," the deputy replied.

"Oh, yeah? take a gander further to the left, where it backs into the boulders. See it, see the smoke?"

"So, that's where they went . . . I wonder if they got any coffee?"

Clifton was straining his eyes to spot anyone, when all at once, two men showed up and headed toward the gate into the corral. Just as suddenly, two more appeared.

"We're just gonna have to wait for for the sheriff and his men to git here," Pea said to Clifton, upon their discovery of the four men. "I never knew there was four men. Hey, Cliff! That corral - you 'spose there's more cows there? can't see 'em all from where we are. You reckon they'd be stolen cows and them guys is . . . is rustlers?"

"Exactly right, partner." Now Clifton was very sure his 'brother', Getwood, was amid them all. After all, they'd followed Croppy's tracks close to the entrance to the Canyon last night, before it got to dark to see. he wanted to go in after them, but Deputy Peabody insisted they wait awhile longer for the posse.

* * *

The incessant rain that drenched the usually arid desert followed the snow and soaked the ground. Then, when the winds changed it was blown further east, and drier weather came in with the dawn.

Hank knew now the tracks were going to his home ranch. He slowed his pace, for he was on his way home to rest his horse.

At least four hours passed since he laid Ranger to rest, to when he rode into his ranch where the outline of the corrals were silhouetted by the sky's first light.

Hank noticed the same big tracks he'd been following appeared near the corral but they disappeared among many others. He put the young horse away, wiped him down and grained him before he headed toward his cabin. He, too, passed the black Morgan in the stall and the buggy in the aisle, and wondered who was here.

Hank was looking for the horse that made the large hoof prints, but it was not in the barn. Jiggs was not among the other horses in the back corral, nor was he in the jingle-horse stall inside the barn, either.

A light or two was showing from the main house and one from his cabin.

Hank guessed someone was starting the breakfast and probably getting ready to go milk the little Guernsey cow he passed at the outer corral.

Hank's thoughts were of Abbey, and he could hardly wait to greet her and crush her softly in his arms. He also wondered just how Aunt Lucy was faring. He thought he would stop at the cabin to see Abbey, and then settle his ravenous appetite with an eagerly awaited,   hearty breakfast, before he took a much needed bath.

Hank was curious who their visitor was, but he was more concerned what had become of the rider whose tracks led him here. He knew there was possible danger and he must find him.

But, where shall he look?

CHAPTER FIFTEEN

THE TRUTH TOLD OF THE PRODIGAL SON

A red winter sun was just starting to poke its warm face from behind the Wassuk Mountains, as Hank stepped on the porch at his cabin and unlatched the door.

"You better be awake, Missy!" Hank laughingly called to Abbey, from the front room.

"I can't stay too long, 'cause . . ."

A frazzled Mary Anne appeared in the bedroom doorway to interrupt the cowboy.

"Hank, thank God."

"Mary Anne! So you're the visitor that's here. Saw the rig in the barn and . . ."

"Hank, it's Abbey, she's . . ."

"Wha-what's going on? What happened?" Hank said, as he rushed past Mary Anne into the bedroom.

His harried, frightened wife, with a terribly swollen face and blackened eye, was sitting on the bed when Hank reached for her.

"Abbey, darlin', what's happened to you?" Hank was looking to Mary Anne now, for any kind of an explanation.

"I-I'm really all right, sweetheart. I've just had a close call with that pitiful idiot, Getwood. He broke in from out of nowhere, about an hour or so ago, and if it hadn't been for Mary Anne, it could have . . ."

"Getwood?" Hank shouted. "Why, that's nearly impossible, unless . . ." suddenly realizing the tracks he followed must have been from a horse Getwood was riding.

But why would he try something like this - and where is he now? He wondered.

"Abbey, for Lord's sake, are you all right? H-h-he didn't . . ."

"He tried," Abbey said, "but he's such a fool and a coward, he only hit me. He left the minute he heard someone calling. I-I thought it might be you. I saved you some supper. I just wanted . . ." She began to softly sob, then tried to hide it from her concerned husband.

Mary Anne then filled Hank in on the whole story, and cautioned that Aunt Lucy was not aware of any of this mess.

As tired and hungry as Hank felt, he was also determined to strike out immediately after his miserable excuse for a 'step-cousin'. The thought that there was kinship between them certainly lost forever, now that Hank was aware of how mean and low a person that Getwood turned out to be.

Mart Anne finally convinced Hank that he should remain with Abbey, at least for a while yet. He could always 'go-after' Get tomorrow.

"Honey," Abbey spoke to her cowboy, "we have to tell Aunt Lucy, sooner or later. I'll tell her the truth, 'cause she's going to wonder what happened to me, but I need you and Mary Anne there, too. This is going to be mighty hard on her. I only wish that Cliff was here, too, at least for her comfort."

Mary Anne helped Abbey dress, while Hank washed himself at the kitchen sink-pump. They all walked next door for the short journey that they all dreaded.

* * *

"Here comes the posse, Cliff." Peabody could see them from his position on the rock ledge of the side entrance to Miller Canyon.

"Boy, I'm near 'bout starved into death. Ain't you hongry, Clifton?"

"I can't find Getwood," Cliff said to the deputy. "He's just not one of those four men. I know I'd recognize him, but he's just not one of those people. Maybe we made a mistake. Maybe there are more than the four, maybe we missed a track. I-I just can't figure it out."

Th deputy wasn't paying Clifton any mind. He climbed down the side of a large boulder that half hid the cave entrance, and began to saddle the horses that were hobbled during the night. Peabody waved his saddle blanket at the men riding up, and Sheriff Sager took off his hat and waved back at him.

"By golly, Pea, there stands ol' Croppy. I knew it was his tracks. I wonder where the hell Getwood is ?" Clifton turned for an answer and saw the deputy gathering the horses.

Everyone of the deputized men were riding in, even Harry Carter. He felt he had an interest because now he was certain some of the cattle they hoped to find were his.

"G'mornin', Sheriff." Deputy Peabody greeted him as the group rode in and began to dismount. "Hope you fellers brought some bait along. We cooked us a couple o'hares last night, and I couldn't git the bad taste outta my mouth. Coffee! Yes sir, that's what I need. You boys surely brought some coffee, right?"

"Yeah, we did." Soapy McClure gave him his answer. "I thought you'd have a cook fire a-goin', Pea. We brought along some biscuits and bacon. None of us has had any breakfast, yet."

"Jim," Cliff said to the sheriff, "there's four men and a corall full of beeves in there."

"Four? Well, there's six of us. Wish Hank would hurry along. That'd help out some. You reckon he is a comin'?"

"Don't know." Cliff retorted. He took the dog and was following a set of tracks heading on back south."

"Well, I'm not sure if there's any other way out of this Canyon, but I do know it's about fifteen miles to the Blackwood siding that feeds into the old S.P. Railroad line to Carson City." Soapy offered this knowledge to anyone who was interested.

"We used that siding three years ago when we gathered the Peterson family's cows that they sold. Some of them wandered into Miller Canyon lookin' for water, 'til they gathered them and pushed them to the siding."

"Well, boys," Sheriff Sager said, "we've got a job to do soon as we're through eatin', so may as well saddle up and get started."

* * *

Myles Cooke and Frank Palmer finally convinced Ren Morgan and Lefty Barker, the seedy rustlers, they all were definitely a part of the new gang that Boyle was forming. The four were already discussing plans of rustling some more cattle in north Mineral county, and points east, too.

"You can always git aholt of your kin at the stock pens in Carson, right?" he said to Lefty. Cooke was positive, but he also questioned him.

"Wul, yeah, I reckon so, 'ceptin' he said last time it was gittin' riskier. He want's a bigger slice of the pie, is all."

"Alls we need to do is find some more of those range cattle over east, cull the ones we want to ship, and we can afford his bigger cut," Ren said, as he started to catch and saddle his big, roan horse.

"Frank, you and Cookie can push drag 'til we git these beeves a-movin'. I'll ride that west flank, and Lefty, you lead out and git that far side corral gate. Push them ol' moss-backs in front, and I'll bet all them yearlin's'll foller 'em."

* * *

Harry Carter and Martin Reyés were on the west side of the arroyo bed, which split the first half-mile of the Canyon. Sheriff Sager and Cliff rode the east side.

Soapy and Peabody started toward the corrals. Each man had his saddle gun out of the scabbard and resting on their thigh, with the hammers cocked. The sun was out in full force and lighted the entire basin.

* * *

Getwood arrived in the outskirts of Carson City about mid-morning on Tuesday and pulled rein at the south-side livery stable, under a freshly-painted sign proclaiming the owner.
"JACOB'S LIVERY STABLE. HORSES &
MULES BOARDED, SOLD & LEASED
TOP FARRIER SERVICE. WELCOME"

Getwood read the entire sign aloud as he stepped down and handed his reins to a huge Dutchman who called himself 'Yake'.

"Ja, ja, oats iss ten cents der gallun, und der keep ober night iss vun dollar for each of der an-i-mools," the Dutchman said, in answer to Getwood's query.

"The Biltmore still a good hotel?" Get asked, "and is the Silver Dollar, still over on third street?"

"Ja, ja. Both iss goot. How long vill you shtay?" Getwood handed the fat man four silver and two paper dollars.

"Be back tomorrow and I'll let you know then. A lot depends . . ."

"Ja? depends on vhat?"

"Depends on whether Big Betty's ladies are still any good, and depends if Dugan's saloon is still in business." He started across the street when Jake said he needed a name to enter on his ledger, and asked what it was.

"Ge . . . uh, Woods. Thomas Woods. I got business with Barney at the stockyards." With this, he hurried on toward

Dugan's to slake his thirst for his gut and gullet, and for his gross indulgence in any carnal pleasures he had.

While he walked, he checked his poke for any money and counted almost one hundred and seventy-two dollars.

* * *

Little Clayton was not a fussy baby. He was content to lie in his crib and play with a few of the toys his grandpa had made for him. His bright-eyed grin greeted his grandmother when she lifted him from the covers of his tiny bed, into the loving rapture of her comforting arms.

"Such a bi-i-g boy, you are sweetheart, grandma loves y . . .gracious! you startled me. What are you doing here, Hank?"

"Aunt Lucy, let Mary Anne hold the baby a moment. Abbey and I have something . . ."

"Abbey!" Lucy shrieked. "What on . . .?"

Fifteen minutes later, the sobbing Aunt Lucy had composed herself, and within a heartbeat was ever so solicitous to Abbey with her condition so apparent.

"You mustn't concern yourself with me," Abbey tried to comfort her. "I really feel much better. I am certain my looks are not as I wish, but I shall soon heal."

"What can I say?" Hank was just as concerned as Mary Anne for Lucy's welfare, and they told her they would do what they could to make her as comfortable as possible.

"Hank, dear, I don't know what I've been thinking - you haven't had a thing to eat, and I know you're just starved. Mary Anne, honey, will you fix the baby's breakfast? I'll start something for Hank."

Lucille Hall was ever the stalwart, pioneer woman with a deep family devotion in her upbringing. Mary Anne knew that Aunt Lucy was deeply, deeply hurt with the finalization of the truth about Getwood's actions toward, not only Abbey, but the lack of any feeling for his brother, and the alienation that came between him and Hank.

It was a difficult story that unfolded from Abbey's lips, but a matriarchal approach demanded that Aunt Lucy would be truly, the strengthening glue to bind her remaining family together. She would put it aside and continue her life on the cow ranch.

Hank returned from the barn with a full pail of milk from the little Guernsey, and placed it in the spring house. The weather was much more pleasant as the day passed, and the ground was rapidly drying from a south-west wind and an all-embracing sun.

Mary Anne finished the washing and hung it from lines strung behind the house to snap dry.

Hank decided he better complete some of the chores that needed doing, especially since he felt Cliff may be gone awhile with the posse.

He needed to put shoes on Duke and on Dobie, and of course, on Lawyer. It could take him several hours to cold-shoe these horses.

He kept on searching for any tracks leading from the barn, especially those of Jiggs and the big-footed horse he tracked in before.

This evening, he'd tell the family about ol' Ranger. Tomorrow, sure, he start out on his search for Getwood.

CHAPTER SIXTEEN

A CONFRONTATION IN MILLER CANYON

Martin Reyés peeled his horse away from beside Harry Carter to ride a little higher above the shale that was forming on his side of the arroyo. His horse climbed almost straight up for about fifty yards, until the land leveled out, and Martin could see further into the Canyon.

There, he saw the dust and heard the soft bawling of cattle that disliked being driven along.

"Amigo mîo," he shouted to Harry. "Aqui, muy pronto." Harry spurred his pony to the same heights as Reyés, and he saw them.

The drovers had to be almost a half-mile ahead of the two posse members, who, by now could make out two riders in the back.

Harry turned his tough, little horse back down and headed straight across the Canyon floor directly for the sheriff and the others.

Harry's stout horse was giving all the heart he had, racing ahead.

Clifton, who was well mounted on the white-footed, sorrel from the livery, and Sheriff Sager, saw Harry riding toward them at a mighty fast pace. He half-turned in his saddle and motioned back south, calling with his arms waving, for Soapy and the deputy to ride up fast.

* * *

Frank Palmer was swinging his grass rope at one of the steers that kept dropping back, attempting to quit the herd. He turned and whistled sharply at the critter and made a pass with his loop.

He missed, and cussed at his failure to pitch slack soon enough. The steer ran back toward the corral area and was heading in the direction of the posse, with Frank Palmer right behind.

The rustler was just about to confront the steer when it jumped to a higher level and passed some outcroppings of rocks. When the horse and rider came up the small plateau, they immediately gazed into the oncoming posse.

The sheriff saw him first and he snapped off two shots, both high and wide. The cartridges caromed off the rock wall and echoed a signal to Cookie, riding up ahead.

Cooke pulled his saddle gun, turned and fired back at an imaginary target, for he could see nothing well, through all the dust.

Deputy Peabody rode his horse east toward where he heard the shots, and where he knew the sheriff was riding. Soapy urged his pony ahead, standing in his stirrups, and firing his rifle at Myles Cooke.

Clifton spotted the rustler about the same time Soapy did, but he hesitated to shoot. He was certain the horse was Croppy, but he couldn't see the rider plain enough to be sure it wasn't Getwood.

Ren Morgan was on the northwest corner and along side the cattle that suddenly spooked, bunched-up and started to run. Not just the faster little trot they do when they're disturbed, but rather, a flat-out run.

Lefty was far enough in the front that when they started their stampede-like running, he got after his horse with all his iron, and spurred him away to the east.

There was a large depression and a number of large boulders about another four hundred yards. The Canyon took a hard turn to the east and continued for several miles in that direction. By now, Ren and Lefty were well aware that they were being followed and who-ever it was, was shooting at them.

Ren Morgan waved at Lefty and motioned him to veer off to the right when they passed the largest of the boulders.

He felt the herd would continue toward the depression and eventually come to the west side of the Canyon's high walls.

Harry Carter, meanwhile, had ridden hard back to the west side of the herd and felt he was gaining on them. Cookie saw him and leveled a shot that Harry felt thwap into the right shoulder of his horse.

He felt the horse's muscles bunch, and with one gasp and a long, loud cough, fold his front feet under and drop to the dusty, sage filled, desert floor.

Harry rolled free and then watched sadly as his stalwart, little horse took his last, brave breath.

The cattle herd was running harder now with the two, older moss-backed cows in front, toward the west wall of the Canyon.

Ren Morgan was frantically attempting to cross between the running steers to reach the opposite side and make the herd turn east, and down the Canyon.

He quickly came upon Harry Carter who was trying to wrestle his saddle loose from under his fallen horse.

"Don't move, feller, or I'll shoot ya where ya stand." Ren's gun was pointed right at Harry.

"You're one of the men that's been stealin' our cattle, ain't ya?" Harry spewed, as he raised his hands higher.

The red-roan horse that Morgan was riding was having a hard time settling down after his fast run through the stampeding cattle, and now being reined down, and made to stand, while Morgan was talking.

Harry quickly used his elbow to smash into the roan's face, causing it to throw its head and rear back, suddenly. The instant this occurred, Harry grabbed the bridle reins and pulled them hard to one side, causing the horse to lose his balance and quickly fall to his side.

When Ren fell from the saddle, Harry then kicked his boot into the rustler's face, smashing his mouth and teeth.

Unknown to either man, both their sidearms were lost when the scuffle began. While Ren was holding his hands to his painful, bleeding mouth, Harry adeptly steeped into the saddle as the roan stood up.

"You darthy bashthard," Ren mumbled from his bloody mouth, holding his hand to his jaw, "you've khiched out all mah teeph."

Harry spurred the roan toward the posse.

Cliff was following the rider on the horse he knew was Croppy, when Harry approached from the side, hollering to Clifton.

"Don't shoot, Cliff. It's me, Harry." he pulled alongside riding Morgan's horse.

"I see you, friend. What's going on? Whose horse? W-what's happening? What is . . ."

"Quick, follow me," Harry told Cliff. "I'll explain on the way." Moments later, the two came on to the downed rustler, who grabbed the rifle from Harry's saddle, and was half-running toward the bend area in the Canyon, where he expected his cohorts to be.

"Stop right there and throw up your hands, Don't make any sudden moves, and get your hand away from your mouth." Clifton directed these words to the outlaw.

Harry stepped down and took the rifle from the rustler, pulled his arms behind his back and tied them with one of the piggin' strings from Morgan's kak.

"What'll we do with him?" Harry asked. "Personally, I'm for shootin the sumbitch."

"The sheriff will be along directly, he'll decide," Cliff answered. "What th'hell happened to your horse, Harry?" Carter explained as the sheriff and his deputy neared.

"Looks like you got one," Sheriff Sager exclaimed. When he was told of the horse situation, he further said, "He'll jut have to walk, I guess, unless we put him on one of our horses, and then ride double."

"Wul, I say he walks," the deputy hollered.

Martin Reyés quietly followed the yearlings to where they were milled-up and beginning to quiet down, along the west base of the Canyon walls, about three miles from where the shooting was taking place.

He gently talked to the beeves, and especially the old moss-backs and the the cow-calf unit, to continue to quiet them. After they settled, he thought they could be pushed back to the corrals for feed and water.

More shots were fired toward the posse, who were gathered closer together in the center of the Canyon floor, from the the east side of the range land. The shots were coming from Frank Palmer, who was riding fast to reach the big bend in the Canyon and catch up with his renegade pals.

There, with good cover, they could easily make a stand. there was timber and water, and the walls would prevent anyone from trying to surround them.

Myles Cooke had the same thoughts. He, too, fired at the group while he was racing across the bottom land to reach his gang at the big bend area.

"Peabody," Sheriff Sager yelled. "Get on up behind Soapy on his big gelding and put this hombré on your horse.

Yonder comes Martin Reyés with them beeves, all as peaceful as a room full of breast-fed babies. Reckon we'll take this feller back to jail in town and let him tell us where them other bad boys was a-headin' with them cows."

The sheriff explained his actions to all his men regarding the abandonment of the rustlers and the posses' return to town.

"Pea, you and Soapy just foller this hombré straight into town, lock him up and get some fresh horses and a few men, and come on back out here and help round-up this gather and put 'em in the town corrals. We can cull 'em out and tally 'em later."

* * *

"What do you make of our crop-eared horse?" Cliff asked the sheriff. "I know it was him, but I'm certain that my brother is not with that bunch, back at the bend."

"I'm not positive, Cliff, but I'd say those tracks you and Pea follered to the Canyon, and then split, was probably caused by your brother switchin' horses with one of them rustlers, and then him tailin' it in the direction that Hank was followin'." The sheriff watched Clifton's reaction very carefully, as he spoke.

Harry Carter and Clifton Hall, along with Martin Reyés and Sheriff Sager, were easily pushing all the cattle to the spot in the Canyon near the front entrance, where they had been held grazing for several weeks, and were comfortable to bed down.

More men would be out later to drive them into the town corrals, the sheriff related.

"I didn't plan on having us ride into any trap today, after them ol' rustlers. We can find out more about them when we start to question the one that we already caught."

CHAPTER SEVENTEEN

A ROUGH TIME IN CARSON CITY

When Hank finished his chores, the next evening, including milking Suzy, the little milk-cow, he watched as the sun settled down and spread its warm, orange and red, and its blue-gray colors behind the mountain range. It was time to prepare for the high-desert night time.

"How're you doin', sweet gal?" Hank asked as he finished toweling the soap and basin water from his face and hands outside their cabin. He stepped onto the old, circular hook-rug of many colors, that lay on the plank floor of their cozy room. "I'm all better, honey," Abbey replied. I feel really good, and you can see all the swelling has gone from my face." Abbey was busy placing another mesquite log in th fireplace, and answered without turning.

"Your cheeks still look a little swollen to me." Hank laughed as he replied, while viewing only the tightness of Abbey's faded blue-jeans, stretched over the roundness of her well-formed bottom.

Abbey whirled with laughter, and their lips met passionately. "Ummm," she said coyly, "You're such a tease."

After only a few moments, Hank returned from the wooden outhouse behind their cabin, stopped to take a long drink of cold water at the kitchen pump by the sink, and headed into their bedroom.

Abbey was already in bed and she had the covers pulled up under her chin. Hank noticed all her clothes were casually draped over the chair back, and then he noticed her impish grin. He quickly undressed and went to their bedside. She lay the covers back with one hand and longingly invited him to climb on in.

"I've counted the hours you were away," she said, "and I'm grateful you chose to follow those tracks back home, darlin'."

"It's just a shame I didn't arrive sooner. I would have killed him, if I had."

"Oh, Hank, let's not discuss the vermin now. I know you'll trail after him tomorrow. Right now, you and I can enjoy what we've missed for a while. Hold me tight, sweetheart, again."

"You betcha," said Hank as he gently lifted her sensuous body closer to his own warm, sleek torso. Their lips met again in a moist repose, and their bodies responded with the wild tremors they both felt.

Abbey was deeply in love with her elegant cowboy, and she felt the passion that she knew was shared between them. Hank's gratification was enormous, and before slumber overtook them both, he told her again, how much he truly did love her.

* * *

Dugan's saloon was across the street from the Silver Dollar Lodging House on Third street, just as Getwood remembered, and directly adjacent from the saloon on Old Barn street, was Big Betty's house of ill repute. Getwood's mind was made up. First, he'd stop at the dram house, then the whore house.

The bar was crowded and warm from the energy created by the patrons. Taggart sat at one of the small, round tables with a saloon gal draped over his lap, and a warm pitcher of suds-less beer on the table.

"Hey, Woods," he called. "Tom Woods! Don'tcha remember me? Percy Taggart! C'mon, and sit down. Have yourself a beer."

"Yeah, I know who you are," Getwood said. "You and Barney run the chutes at the stock yards. I'm surprised you remember me, although you should be gettin' a car load of quality beeves in afore noon tomorrow. They should make you a whole lotta money."

"As long as you get the paperwork handled, we'll cut you a check, and re-routed to Laramie. The big boss has three more carloads arriving' tomorrow, 'bout the same time."

"Yeah, well Taggart, I may not be there just first thing tomorrow. I got me some plans, but I'll see you both a'fore noon, that's when I expect my shipment. You tell Barney to have my check ready. Now, I'll have that beer - to start."

All the money he could find was the twelve dollars in paper he had stuffed in his left boot. He didn't remember that 'Big Betty', herself, dragged him from her place to the Silver Dollar, registered for him, and half-carried him back to room number four, on the first floor, under the stairway.

She had an absolute rule that no 'patron' stayed at her place throughout the entire night.

His head was bursting with a pulsating throb that was only interrupted by his vomiting several times, He drank all the water from the night stand pitcher, and tilted the whiskey bottle to drain the last drop or two.

Getwood fell back across the bed and felt the swirling sensation of the room spin, then he finished disgorging again.

Two more hours of drunken slumber kept Getwood from appearing at the tub room down the hallway. He did finally stumble carefully to the door and call the attendant to fill the wooden tub so he could take a very much needed bath.

He paid the kid a dollar to fetch his clean clothes from his bedroll-pack, stored at the livery stable. Now he had only eleven left. This would be enough to pay his room bill and get something to eat.

After his mid-morning meal he headed back to Big Betty's'. This time to combat Marcie Mae. He was almost certain she'd robbed him of his money poke, and he didn't remember if she even kissed him, either.

"Well-ll, " said Big Betty. "Look who is back for seconds! I didn't think I'd see you before another day or two of hibernation', you 'bad bear, you."

"I'm lookin' for Marcie Mae. She robbed me, you know?"

"Look, Woodsie-baby, I don't know how much money you had when you came in here but I do know you were packing a pretty good load of Dugan's booze. And another thing, if you're lookin' for Marcie Mae, you can just come back. Today's her day off, and she's probably spendin' her hard earned cash up town at the 'Bon-Ton'."

Big Betty said all this while standing in her doorway with her big arms folded.

"Well," said Getwood, "I ain't gonna let this slide, but I got bid'ness to do." He pivoted on his boot heel and headed for the livery, before going to meet Barney and Taggart at the pens.

"Gooten morg'n," Big Jake said, as Getwood sore-footed it toward the stable. "You haff a goot night, ja?"

"Just get my gray ready for me Dutch, I'm headin' fer the registrar's office, and then over to the stockyards. I'll be back to pick up my other horse later on."

"Ja, ja," Jake laughed, as he said, "I seen der boy whut cooms to get der closse you vare. A wery goot night, ja?"

* * *

"Got all your paperwork with you, Woods?" Taggart said to Getwood, who rode his new gray to the front gate at the town stock pens. There were already two of the lots filled with cattle, watering at the log troughs.

Another shipment was unloading about a half-mile up the track siding, at the west end of the stockyards.

"I got everything in order," replied Getwood.

"That my shipment comin' in, yonder?"

"No, that's' them Cromwell ranch beeves. They're from over east of Elko. Left Monday," Taggart answered Getwood.

"Yours ain't here yet, Woods," said Barney, as he rode up during the conversation. "I had them figured to get here late this mornin'. Maybe they had some trouble a-loadin' 'em. I'll check with the dispatcher after while. Give 'em some time, yet. You got the two sets of forms like I told ya?"

"Everything's all set. Just get my check ready so I can get to the Stockman's Bank a'fore they close up."

"Say, Woods," Barney queried. "You got a way to keep this, uh- little enterprise a'goin'?"

"You bet. This ain't the best place to discuss it, but I'm startin' a bid'ness with, shall we say, a couple of new partners. We should be able to supply you with all the 'merchandise' you can handle and ship out."

"Tell your big boss that Lefty is still with me, too. . . .Where the hell's that train car?" Getwood nervously repeated.

The jail at Walker Lake was occupied by two men, now that Morgan, the rustler had been placed in the cell next to the town's drunk, Rufus Higgenbotham. Rufus most always spent one night in jail and sometimes, if he caused the merchants too much trouble, two nights.

"You're mah new neighbor, hic, ain't cha?" Rufus greeted Ren Morgan, as Deputy Peabody locked the cell and took the key ring to the desk in the front room.

"Nether mind a-talkin'." Ren answered surly, his mouth still painfully sore from the missing teeth that were kicked out of his mouth by Harry Carter. "All I neep is mah phartner t'git here frum Carthun, an he'll sphring me outta here. They cain't hol' me."

* * *

Clifton told the sheriff that since they didn't find his brother, he'd like to question the prisoner on what he might know about Getwood, as soon as they reach town.

"I believe I'll just ride on home, Jim. See if I can cut Hank's tracks, or, if not, I know Momma will want to know more about this mess. You'll take care of Morgan?"

"You bet, Cliff," he answered. "I aim to question our prisoner and I intend to get some answers, too. So, you just go ahead and I'll be sure to get word to you if anything's new."

As Cliff was parting company, the sheriff called to him and said, "The boys will bring the cattle in and we'll feed yours 'til you're ready to move 'em. Tell your mother how sorry I am about all this, and for her not to worry, we'll get it all straightened out."

Clifton was riding the white-footed sorrel that he saddled at the livery, and on his way back he was figuring that he would return this horse and pick up the sorrel team tomorrow. Since he hadn't talked to Caleb or his mother about his Dad's funeral plans, he was sure they'd wait until Sunday. He reined his horse for the Circle Diamond, and placed him in an easy, dog-trot gait.

* * *

Hank rode Lawyer back to the barn after he'd only been gone long enough to finally cut the tracks he'd seen when he came in the other day. They were the same horses, but it looked as though Jiggs was being ridden this time. The other was likely being used as a pack animal.

As Hank was crossing from the barn toward his cabin, he saw Cliff, riding in.

"What's going on?" They simultaneously said, to one another, and then laughed at their greetings.

Hank informed his cousin of the miserable events that took place the day before yesterday. Clifton was livid when he heard about Getwood. "Does Mother know?" He painfully awaited

Hank's answer. "After all that she's been through! I suppose you talked over the funeral arrangements, what do you think she wants to do?"

"I'm mighty glad you're here," said Hank, "we'll just have to have a family discussion on this, 'cause I think the tracks I found are most likely headed for Carson City."

* * *

In the parlor, inside the house, Mary Anne was busy talking to, and rocking, little Clayton Hall, when his father and Hank entered. She stood and handed Clifton his happy baby boy.

"What great caretakers you and Abbey are. You help Mom so much when you watch out for Cody, and, Mary Anne, I especially want you to know how much I truly appreciate it."

Clifton was enjoying his son, when his mother came into the room and informed everyone it was feeding time for Clayton. She kissed her son hello, and took the baby with her to the kitchen. "I'll visit with you at supper."

Mary Anne casually drifted onto the front porch when Cliff walked there and removed the sack of 'Bull Durham' and the papers to roll a smoke.

"Here, let me do that, Cliff," she said, as she tapped the tobacco into the paper that she held between her thumb and two fingers. The early evening was warming, as she inched closer to place the cigarette she made, between Cliff's half-open lips.

"You're not only good with my boy, Mary Anne, you're good with my makins', too. You sure make me feel comfortable, just bein' near you . . .uh . . . I, uh, it's been a . . ."

"Don't talk, sweet guy. I know you have needs, same as I do. I've always admired you, and I know what a good man you are. It probably feels awkward for us to be . . ."

Cliff pulled her soft, warm body closer to his chest and wrapped his arms around her magnificent body, before he kissed her sweet lips with the fervency of a passionate and very caring man who missed his wife, terribly.

"Maybe we shouldn't be . . ."

"Nonsense," Cliff hushed her with a longer, more meaningful kiss. "We're adult people who can love one another, and make some right decisions for our future."

"Clifton Hall, what are you saying? Do you realize ? Oh, Cliff, my past . . ."

"All I know, is that you've been a wonderful friend to Abbey, and Hank thinks the world of you. You've always been more than gracious to me, since we've known one another. You have always been there for people in a crisis, and this tells me a whole lot about your character, You're wonderful to Cody, and he adores you."

"Oh, Cliff, I don't know what to say. You're good for me, but I'm in a very difficult job. I can't possibly continue under this context."

"Listen, Mary Anne, I realize everything's happening mighty fast, but just for a moment, think about the future you and I could have together, here, on the Circle Diamond, with Abbey and Hank and a ranch that's as good or better'n most. It would just work perfectly."

"Oh, Cliff," she said, with tears of happiness in her otherwise limpid green eyes. "I love you so very much, and I know I need you. Please, please kiss me once more and hold me tight. I-I'm just . . ."

"Mary me, oh, marry me, and I'll take care of you, I promise. We'll take care of each other. . . . Oh, Mary Anne, be my wife."

They had only a few moments more together, on the porch, before they heard Aunt Lucy announce that supper was on the table.

CHAPTER EIGHTEEN

A SURPRISE FOR THE FAMILY

Myles Cooke already had his .52 caliber, M1859 'Sharps' carbine pulled, and Frank and Lefty watched as Cookie reined Jiggs to a sliding stop and stepped off the sweat-stained horse.

He was as mad as a bee-stung mule. "It's yer fault, you jug-haid, you." He was directing his frothy temper to Frank Palmer. "If you'd stayed with the herd on that side, we could've turned 'em. Now we've lost 'em, and we've lost any chance of gettin' 'em to the siding."

"Take it easy, Myles," Palmer answered. "They ain't that far ahead, we could . . ."

"You crazy, Palmer?" Lefty spoke up. "There's no way the three of us could beat that posse, turn the herd around, and still get 'em o the siding in time. No way!"

"He's right, Myles. Let's get outta here, and ride back to the Dixon shack. Getwood will meet us there with a different plan, soon's he finds out they ain't no shipment comin' to Carson."

"He'll be madder'n a snake-bit bull," Frank said, "'bout all this, 'specially when he finds out they got ol' Morgan." The men grumbled among themselves, but only for a few moments. They wisely decided to get away from the Canyon and go to the shack, but also decided to wait for the darkness to arrive - in case the posse was watching.

Soon, the three left the big bend area, and searched for their exit from Miller Canyon.

* * *

Getwood couldn't understand it. Each and every detail had been carefully planned, with the exception of the two robbers. But they decided to join up with his gang and could be a big help in moving all the rustled cattle.

"Where could they be? What th-hell's happened?" He thought, aloud.

"Well, Woods, that's it. We're a-shuttin' down for the night. We open at six tomorrow," Barney shouted to Getwood. Taggart and he were both dismounting, and about to put their feed-lot horses away.

"You positive that's the last shipment of rail cars you're expectin' today? There's been some mistake made by them railroaders. They better not be more'n two days. I can't have them beeves losin' travelin' weight."

"Take it easy, Woods. There ain't nuthin' we can do 'bout nuthin'. That ain't any of our problems," Barney told Getwood, in plain terms. "You're the one with the problem. We got us a contract from you to supply the big bosses with 20,000 pounds of beef on the hoof. You don't furnish it, you don't get paid, we don't make money and you have got the problem."

"Well, maybe my boys had some kind'a trouble movin' them steers, or maybe they had loadin' problems. I paid for that rail car to be there, so they'll just have to wait for the load. I'll give 'em another day." Get wearily replied.

* * *

Deputy Peabody unlocked the cell where Rufus was and told him to get up and leave. "The sheriff told me to be sure to let you go when I locked your neighbor, here, in our deluxe accommodations. Sheriff don't want his wife to have to cook for both of you, so you're on your own, Higgenbotham."

The stage from Hawthorne was stopped in the street in front of the Palace Hotel. Discharged passengers departed and the young Howe kid was helping Jack Simms disperse the mail.

"Mornin', Deputy," Billy Howe said, as he handed a few letters and a stack of papers to Deputy Peabody.

"Thanks, Billy, I see we got some 'desperado pitchers' here, reckon I best nail 'em up, afore the sheriff gits back."

"I can do that fer ye, fer a dollar." Peabody looked around suddenly, and there stood Rufus, with a grin on his face, mostly hidden by his long red beard.

"Here," said the deputy, as he handed him the posters and the hammer. "Be sure to finish nailin' 'em before you head for the Lucky Partner." Rufus didn't respond. He just grinned again, and held open his palm for the dollar, and then he would be able to quaff a few drinks.

Soapy McClure rode up to the front of the jail with three cowboys from the RXR ranch and a vaquéro from the Box K, ready to meet and bring in the herd.

"Okay, Deputy. we're ready to go after all those yearlings at Miller Canyon."

* * *

Harry Carter wasn't real comfortable on the roan horse he was riding, although he figured he'd get used to him, and he got him fair and square. After all, he lost his own horse to the outlaw's bullets, and he was with the sheriff when they captured the roan horse's owner. At any rate, he was helping Martin Reyés and the sheriff with the herd on their way back to Walker Lake.

"Yonder comes some men," said Harry. "There' Soapy and Peabody and four more."

¿Mas ganado? Reyés questioned, as he pointed along the base at the east side of the canyon.

"You're right, Martin. there are more beeves over there. I was almost certain there were more than just this jerk we have here. I'd guess now, that these were just a part to fill out a load to be sold somewhere, possibly Carson City." Sheriff Sager was telling this to the rest who, by now , had joined the drive.

"I 'spect we'd better all line out and circle back and around. There's got to be more of 'em here in this canyon."

"Let's let the RXR boys round 'em up, they should know this canyon, their ranch borders it on the north. Soapy, you and I, and Peabody can start these beeves on toward town, along with Harry."

"I'm ridin' with Reyés, Jim, and the vaqüero" Harry said, as he reined his newly acquired roan horse, toward the cliffs.

* * *

"Son, you're just picking at your food. Is there something wrong with it?" Aunt Lucy looked a bit disappointed, as she questioned her son. "And you have been grinning from the moment you came in and sat down. Now, what in the world is going on?"

"Mary Anne, dear, " Abbey said to her, "you are just as bad as Cliff, Just what *is* going on? You hav . . . oh, my God! Now I know - I've been watching since you and Cliff walked in . . .oh, oh Mary Aaa-nnne!!"

Clifton scooted his chair back, rose, and put one arm around Mary Anne's shoulder, and his other hand in his mother's palm.

"Listen, Mother, Abbey, Hank- there's some-thing you all should know. I-I've asked Mary Anne to become my wife, to live here, to share my life, and become a part of our family, I-I want you all to . . ."

"There's no need to stammer, son. I fully approve," his mother said. "Go on, and kiss her, and then let Mary Anne have a say."

Abbey bolted from her seat and raced around the table to hug her best friend, amid loud squeals of joy.

"I hope you realize how thrilled and excited I am. I always admired Cliff, now I have fallen totally, and helplessly in love with him. I-I know it seems a little soon . . .well, a lot's happening right now, and . . . "

"Now the same goes for you, honey," Aunt Lucy said. "No need for you to stammer, or be embarrassed. You both have my blessing and all the love our family can bestow."

Hank wasn't totally taken aback by Clifton's sudden announcement. He thought a great deal of Mary Anne, and he was certain that Cliff was doing the correct thing.

He felt what other folks may think might upset Aunt Lucy some, and turn a few heads among several of the town's gossips, but he also knew the caliber of stock his aunt was made of and decided not to give it another thought. The main thing was that both Cliff and Mary Anne would be happy. He knew they'd prosper over the years, for the ranch was a very profitable outfit.

On the front porch, after supper, Hank was talking to Clifton. "You know what, old friend? I'm right proud of your decision and I think Mary Anne will be a mighty fine addition to our family, here at the Circle Diamond."

Clifton was 'rolling-a-cob' from one foot to another, grinning from ear to ear, and trying to build a smoke as he listened to his cousin and best pal.

"I appreciate what you said, Hank. I know there's a few things that need to be straightened out before Mary Anne and I both hitch up double. We have to take care of my Daddy's funeral, and be certain Ma will be all right, and then there's this nasty matter of my brother and his gang an . . ."

"He's your adopted brother, Cliff. He isn't blood you know, and he's gonna get what's coming to him if I have my way. I'm not forgiving him for what he tried to do with Abbey, let alone his rustling capers.

You and I are going after him tomorrow!"

CHAPTER NINETEEN

THE PINKERTON AGENCY INFORMATION

The RXR ranch cowboys were sure they had all of the maverick and rustled cattle bunched with the herd that Soapy McClure, Deputy Peabody and Sheriff Sager were busy pushing through town toward the corrals.

"Let's go ahead, Pea, you and me," the sheriff said. "Here comes Reyés and the Box K cowboy, and Harry Carter with nine or ten more. We're winding up with about all the county's rustled cattle.

Deputy Peabody was busy telling the sheriff all about the goin's on in town, from when he left that morning to now, as they rode together.

". . .and I turned Rufus loose, just as you said to do, so's your wife don't have to feed him and the new man, too."

"Did you fill out all the paperwork for the new men that joined our posse? You know that Meskin from the Box K, and the three cowboys from the RXR ranch, too?" Jim asked.

Jim Sager was sure Peabody had not filled in the paperwork on the new men, but he quizzed him anyway.

"Oh, I reckon I fergot to tell ya. We got us a new batch of 'wanted posters', the stage delivered." Pea rambled on and on.

"I'm hopin' we got some information on the Farris feller, and on this last one we captured back there, in the canyon," Jim said to Peabody.

"If we get some background information on those bozos, as well as some 'wanted' pictures to nail up, it'll help us to solve who's behind this."

"Boy, it shore feels good to git off mah saddle fer awhile," Peabody remarked, as he sorted through the paperwork that lay on the desk inside the jail house. "This here what you're a-lookin' fer, Jim? He handed some letters and more information to him. "This letter's marked personal. Says right here on the envelope, see?"

PINKERTON DETECTIVE AGENCY, INC.
312 Blocker Street, Rm. 106
West Division Headquarters
CARSON CITY, LYON CO., NEVADA
To: J. Sager, Sheriff, Mineral Co., Nevada
From: A. Moore, Commanding, Post # 12
Re: FERRIS, HOLDEN, a.k.a. WHEELER,Wm.
   * Dishonorable discharge, (sec.6-a 13)
     from Conf.Sts.of Am., 2nd Georgia
     Inf., 30 Mar. '82, Athens, Ga.
   * Nevada St, Prison, Carson City, Nev.
     term: 6 yrs. 6 mos.. (sec.14-c 07)
   * Elko, Nev. Jail. robbery (sec. 14-b)
     10 Aug. '75-10 Oct. '75. Abetting
     Claremore gang: robbery (sec.14-d)

Re: BOYLE, FRANKLIN, a.k.a. HALL, GETWOOD
   * Nevada St. Prison, Carson City, Nev.
     term: (12) Twelve Years, four days.
     (sec. 36, code 4) Homicide. 2nd deg.
     04 Jan. '74 - 03 Jan.'86 . . . .

"Here's another one , Sheriff," the deputy said, as he tore the top from the envelope before handing it to the sheriff.

"Let me have that, Pea. I can open my own mail, ya know? This is a follow-up on the first one you opened," Jim said.

"Looks like it's some information on that bird in the back cage. Let's see."

PINKERTON DETECTIVE AGENCY, INC.
312 Blocker Street. Room 106
West Division Headquarters
CARSON CITY, Lyon Co., NEVADA
To: J. Sager, Sheriff, Mineral Co., Nevada
From: A. MOORE, Commanding, Post #12
Re: MORGAN, RENNAN THEADORE (no alias)
* Dishonorable Discharge, (sec.6-a132)
from Conf. Sts. of Am. 2nd Georgia
Infantry Div. Dchg date: 15 Mar. '62
* Wyoming St. Prison, Rawlins, Wyo.
term: (4) Four years, (1) one day.
conv. art. #31-5, cattle rustling.

"Well, it looks as though we might have an ex-convict that's already served a time for cattle stealing in Wyoming, and who was dishonorably discharged from the Confederate Army back in 1862," remarked the sheriff.

"I never knew Lucille's boy served any hard time, I guess ol' Clyde kept that from me. Poor Lucille. All right, Morgan, you best give me some information on your pal, Getwood Hall."

"Ith he here? Tell 'im ah neep ta thee 'im." Morgan's mouth was mighty sore.

"No! He's not here. You tell me what you both have going on, and where he is." The sheriff continued, "It 'pears to me, you got a chance of getting out of here if you cooperate. You served time for your rustling, according to all the official reports from Carson City."

"I may decide to . . . let's say . . . exchange what I think is a rustling scheme in which you may or may not be involved, for you a-tellin' us here the whereabouts of this Getwood Hall, and just what he means to you. You know he often uses a different name, too?"

"You mean you'd lep me go iph as tell ya 'bout thhiss Hall fella? Ren lisped. "Wal, heeph th' one thass rethponsibl' fer causin' us to haff ta move a few cows, jus ta thurvive, ya know? He's gop cannecthshuns at the sthoff pens in Carthun Thity, an he promithed ups big money if we'ud gapther a few beefths that belonged to hith ranch . . . said they'ud never mith 'em."

"Well, where can we find him?" the sheriff pressed on. "What were you going to do with the cows we caught you with? Where were you taking them? Was Hall going to meet you some-where? Better give us some good answers, and be quick about it, too."

During the next half-hour, Sheriff Sager and Deputy Peabody finally raised some answers to their questions to Morgan.

"Okay," Morgan said. "Lep me go now, Shuriff."

"Not so fast, I said I'd exchange with you, but I have to keep you here 'til I get some answers back with my reports from Carson, according to the law." Sheriff Sager told his prisoner, as he winked to Peabody.

* * *

The second day passed and there was absolutely no rail car with an allotment of beeves assigned to a Thomas Woods. Six more shipments had arrived, but none were marked for Getwood to receive.

"Somethin's gone wrong, fer sure," Getwood said, to one of the men he was to do some business with, at the rail siding pens.

"Yeah, well there ain't nuthin' we can do about it, now is there, Mister Woods?"

Barney was half-mad at Getwood, because he wasn't certain that the man could straighten it out, and he feared that he was going to lose money for his part of the plan.

"I'm just gonna have to pull out now and get this mess lined up," Getwood said. "I'm sure we'll be doin' business real soon, though. I'll have Lefty get in touch with you, Barney, afore this week's over."

Percy Taggart rode up as the two men were finishing their conversation, and asked Getwood what he was going to do.

"I just told Barney, here, that I intend to find out what happened to my shipment. I ne..."

"Our shipment, Woods!"

"Yeah, . . . our shipment. Like I said, I'm on my way to meet with my 'boys', and arrange a brand new car load just as soon as possible. It ain't like we have to requisition cattle, 'cause we already got 'em hid out. We just have to get 'em loaded and delivered, right?"

On his way over from the stock pens to Jake's livery stable, Getwood was swearing aloud and spurring ol' Blue, the dapple-gray that once belonged to Myles.

"Be damned! I can't trust that Ren or Lefty to do anything right. Hope t-hell them new boys ain't fouled anythin' up; I ain't too certain of all them, neither. Wal, guess I'll just have to ride on back to the cabin. Reckon that's where they'll likely be. They'll be waitin' fer me to git there and tell 'em what to do next, Gid-yap, Blue."

* * *

"Ja, ja, iss goot to shee you, all oop soober und riding dot ghray hars, You owe me turty-two dollar more, ja, und I keep your udder hars, if you not pay to me, ja?"

"Look, Dutch," Get replied, "I didn't get paid my money from the stock pens, and I ain't got time to explain any more to you. I need my sorrel pack horse now, and I'll be on my way. I'll pay you when I get back."

"Ach! No! you pay me now," Jake said, as he reached up and jerked Get from his saddle and onto the stable dirt. There was no one to witness this, so Getwood pulled his side gun when Jake reached down to grab him.

"You made a bad move, Dutch, and I'll drill a hole in the middle of your big belly. Now, back up and git Jiggs ready to travel. Do it now."

Big Jake did as he was told. "You make big mishtaken, " Jake growled, when he handed him the halter rope.

"Look, Dutch, I'm sorry, 'bout this, but I have to get my business taken care of. I'll be back and pay you what I owe you, and I may pay you double, 'cause I'm gonna have more money than you can think of . . .soon, trust me.

Getwood snickered to himself when he said this, as he rode out toward the Dixon shack - to look for some answers.

Somehow, Jake felt he'd never see this man again, He shrugged and turned away.

CHAPTER TWENTY

AN ESCAPE FROM THE PIAUTES

Everyone at the Circle Diamond cow ranch woke to a glorious sunrise with garnet and lemon colored clouds in a soft, cerulean blue sky. The morning chores were finished quickly, and Hank and Clifton headed over to the main house to share another one of Aunt Lucy's most comforting breakfasts'.

"Those tracks I told you about were leading in the direction to the road to Carson City. I'm just sure that's where he went." Hank said.

"I intend to ride Lawyer, and I s'pose you'll saddle up ol' Dobie."

"That's my intention, Hank. I guess we should leave as soon after breakfast as we can. The weather is sure co-operatin'."

They both stopped to wash at the basin on the front porch.

"I smell hog-sausage frying," Cliff said, as he handed the towel to Hank.

* * *

Getwood was furious when he spied the horses in the pole corral by the cabin at the Dixon property. He looked again and noticed the roan horse Ren was riding was not out there.

Lefty's pinto, and Palmer's bay horse and the crop-eared sorrel that Cookie was riding, were the only ones he saw. He took the lead rope from Jiggs and stepped off the gray, to unsaddle, and placed these two in the corral.

"What in the blue blazes happened?" Get shouted, as he flung the cabin door open and entered the room. Lefty and Palmer jumped up from their chairs as soon as Getwood spoke, but Cookie remained seated and put his hands up and out, palm open, to quiet Getwood.

"Hold on there, Boyle. We've been through a time with them beeves, and from that posse that found us."

"Whutter-you talkin' 'bout?" Hall replied. What posse . . . where? I want answers. You dummies has cost me a lot of money, so talk."

Finally, Getwood was assured reasons the shipment didn't come was due to facts his gang related. They told him the sheriff had Ren, and Get decided they'd devise a plan to get him out of jail. "'Nother thing, get me some of that bank money, I'm broke."

* * *

Hank and Clifton were on their way to Carson City, where they would begin their search for Getwood. The weather was good, no clouds in the day sky, as Clifton spoke up.

"We can't stay too long in Carson, Hank. We simply have to get back to Walker Lake and make those funeral arrangements."

"Abbey and Mary Anne are going to handle it, Cliff. I talked to her about it this morning. They're setting it up for next Tuesday, provided Aunt Lucy approves of the . . ."

"Oh, she will," Cliff interrupted. "She'll listen to Mary Anne and Abbey, for sure. We just have to plan to be on time, that's all. Right?. . . wh-what . . .Hank?"

"Don't turn around, keep ridin' and lookin' straight ahead. We've got to make it past those outcroppings of rocks up ahead, and through those trees."

"For Pete's sake, Hank . . ." and then he saw them. He remembered now, the sheriff mentioned an uprising that could happen from the Piautes. They held the land the railroad was using to bring more miners into this part of the state territory.

"There's probably twenty or more up there on the ridge," Hank exclaimed. "Whoops! There's another group across the ravine. How many you make there?"

"About twelve or thirteen. What d'ya suppose caused this mess, anyway? And how'd we get in the middle? Oh, no! They're Piautes - and they're likely painted, too."

The two men literally rode for their lives. The Indians were attempting to surround them for reasons unknown to the cowboys, so they desperately needed to effect an escape. The distance between the cowboys and the screaming Indians was likely more than a mile, and a five minute start.

Hank felt this would give them more than enough time to get across the back side of the ravine and up into the white sage that covered the flat land leading to the Carson City road.

They raced their horses for the open road where they knew the footing was better. There would be no way the Indians had any horses that were capable of catching the two Hank and Cliff were riding. Mostly, those Piaute horses were of a shorter leg, and smaller statue, and certainly not as well bred as the Circle Diamond horses.

The leader of the painted raiders carefully split his forces, but failed to anticipate their quarry doubling back the way the Hall's did. This probably cost the Indians another ten minutes and two miles.

When Hank and Cliff reached the main road, they followed it a good mile or so, before it turned and tumbled into a rockier terrain where outcroppings of large boulders began to appear.

Here, they left the road and headed toward the rocks. Sure to cause them slower going, but very, very hard to be tracked. By now, it looked as though the two had momentarily escaped their adversaries.

"I can't believe those Piautes were only after us," Cliff said. "There's some reason for them to be on a raid all painted and wearing their ceremonial 'war' bonnets."

"Not sure they were after just you and me, just look over there at the Jenson ranch. See the smoke? We're probably too late, Cliff. maybe we should ride for the fort and let Colonel Davis know about this, if he doesn't already know."

"You're right, Hank. It's only four miles to the fort from Jensons'. They surely can see the smoke from their high ground, so let's ride!"

"Go ahead, Cliff, fast as you can. I'm gonna ride over to see what's left of their ranch. From here, the only animal I can see is Ezra's white mule runnin' 'round and 'round in their south corral. Damn Injuns musta stole the rest of the horses. When you reach the fort, tell 'em to bring along a doctor."

The two parted company, and Clifton hadn't ridden a mile before he spotted the squad of cavalry and a wagon heading toward Jensons'. He pulled rein and talked to the young, second Lieutenant, about all the events that occurred within the last half hour.

"Corporal O'Malley," the officer barked. "Get to the fort immediately with this message about the red men Mister Hall has identified as Piautes, and the fire at the ranch. I'll take the detail to ascertain any damage and casualties, Move out!"

"Yes, sir," was accompanied by a very snappy salute, as the corporal spurred away.

Hank arrived at the Jenson corrals, which were all that was standing from this terrible fire. He wondered why the mule was still running back and forth in the corral, when the pole bars that formed a gate were strewn down.

Hank tied Lawyer to a corner post and tossed a head rope on the mule. The mule was still trembling as Hank started to gentle him down, when he exclaimed,"Damn, he's blind."

Martha Jenson never had a chance. Hank found her terribly charred body with all her clothes burned off, slumped over her rifle. She had four, long arrows impaled in her chest and shoulder. After an extensive search, Ezra was nowhere to be found.

Hank finished digging the grave and he was carefully placing the hard Nevada earth over Martha's body when he saw troopers arriving with Clifton. "That was mighty quick," he thought to himself, 'til Cliff later explained his meeting the soldiers on the road.

The next thirty minutes was spent by everyone searching a wider area looking for Ezra. The officer felt he may have crawled away and was hiding in on of the ditches.

Clifton and Hank discussed the possibility that Ezra wasn't even present when the raid occurred. There was no sign of his wagon anywhere, even any burned pieces.

Trooper Wyatt approached with the report that two soldiers had just discovered the remains of Jenson's two dogs . . . butchered.

* * *

"Hü, " cried El Ladrøn, as he reined his war pony to a full stop. Arbøl Colorådo joined him.

"Hü," he answered. In two minutes the entire war party of Northern Piautes had assembled when El Ladrøn motioned with his sacred war lance for all to gather.

He spoke to Red Tree.

"Hear me, Arbøl Colorådo. It is growing late and we will move to the river bank and make camp at the place on side where sun sets. The pony soldiers will be alerted by smoke left at ranchero where we get these seven horses. They will be fooled by tracks our scouts make. They think we ride to white Wassuk mountains."

Many of the Piautes were young men, just past boyhood, and they were still full of energy and ready for a fight with the pony soldiers.

El Ladrøn, was also known as 'The Robber'. He slid off his horse and walked to to three young men he felt disobeyed his words to not pursue the two white men past the road to white-eyes big camp, *'Kar-sun-Ci-ty'.*

"You will not be permitted to count coups, when we engage soldiers," he told them. "You will ride inside circle, and when we camp you are responsible for wood and water. No more talk."

* * *

"I'm sorry to disagree with you, Lieutenant" said Hank. "But, I'm certain those Indians are not headed toward the Wassucks. Those are probably false tracks, and not nearly enough at that. Cliff and I met a war party of more than thirty braves south of here. They've got to be responsible for the death of Missus Jenson, as well as the fire."

"You positive of that, Mister Hall?"

"You bet."

"How'd you escape thirty Indians?"

"We doubled back, Lieutenant," Cliff replied to his question. "This clay-bank horse of mine, and Hank's bay can outrun those puny Injun ponies any day of the week. That's when we saw the Jenson ranch fire."

"Trooper Redhorse, front and center," called the Lieutenant. After conferring with the soldier, who was a full-blooded Umitila, and the best scout-tracker at the fort, the officer deferred to both the cowboys, that their theory of false tracks was entirely correct.

"The question is, gentlemen, in which direction are these renegades deploying? I realize the urgency of a quick follow-up is necessary, but unfortunately, my orders only cover the consequences of the smoke we saw from the fort. We are only to investigate and then secure that which is pertinent to that very task."

Hank looked in wonderment, at first to Cliff, and then, while shaking his head, to the officer.

"We have urgent business in Carson City, Lieutenant," Clifton said, when he was finishing tightening the cinch on 'Dobie.

"Personal family business," Hank reiterated while he mounted his bay horse, of whom he was so fond.

"It's only my opinion, Lieutenant, but you'd better make fast tracks for Fort Carson. With this one band of Piautes looking for a fight, that we escaped, there's bound to be more on the war path, nearby."

"We're about to do that very maneuver," the officer replied. "My orders are not to engage any hostiles; however, Colonel Davis must be made aware of the Indian moves taking place. We hurry, we'll make it back before tattoo. Sergeant, form the detail. Prepare to mount - mount! Column of two's fo-oard, ho."

Hank and Cliff had about another two hours ride before they'd arrive in Carson City. They both had second thoughts about their task at hand, knowing the women were at the ranch alone, and the rest of the hands were on the range. "Mary Anne and Abbey are capable and they'll watch out for your mom," Hank said.

"Cliff!"

"Yeah, Hank?"

"We're sure lucky, to have such good horses, and good women."

CHAPTER TWENTY ONE

THE COWBOYS SEEK SOME ANSWERS

Clifton handed the Dutchman a five dollar gold piece, and four dollars in paper.

"We know it's late and we're headed for the Silver Dollar lodging house. The extra money is for you to rub down both our horses real good, and toss some rolled oats along with their hay, tonight. We rode 'em pretty hard today. We'll most likely get 'em after breakfast, in the morning."

"Ja, ja," Jake replied. "I tak dem sum goot care uff, und rob 'em down, too, ja, ja. Tanks."

"You reckon the Silver Dollar is still open for bait and a room?" asked Hank.

"Ja, ja. Thurd shtreet, ja."

"Really," Hank grinned. See ya."

It was about twenty past five the next morning, and a briskness was in the early air. Dawn was slow in arriving when Hank and Clifton approached the east gate to the stockyards.

"Figure this is as good a place to start as any, lookin' for that no-good,'step' brother of yours, Cliff. When these fellers get to work we'll ask 'em what they know about a car load of beeves shipped to a Getwood Hall from . . where, I don't know?"

"Maybe they'd be under the name of that Ferris fella that died from the blood poisoning in our shoot-out last month."

"Don't forget that Lefty Barker has a cohort that's s'posed to be working here, too."

Percy Taggart was the first one to arrive, and was so busy forking hay to to the five, feed-lot horses that he failed to notice Clifton and Hank. The two men were sitting atop the pole logs that formed an outside of the east end of the barrier, and they were straddling the round logs.

"G'mornin', mister." Cliff said, as he used his teeth to pull on the tag at the top of his tobacco sack. "You're startin' chores early." He spoke louder as he proceeded to roll the smoke.

Taggart nearly jumped from his skin, while dropping the hay fork, and expounding expletives.

"Jae-sus, you boys scairt the fool outta me."

"Sorry, friend," Hank said. "We're here to find a feller we think is meetin' a car load or two of beeves. Maybe you know of him" Name's Getwood Hall."

"No, it don't sound familiar, but Barney's due here any minute now, and he probably knows him. How many cars did ya say?"

"Don't know for sure, but this would be the right place to unload and sell, now, wouldn't it?"

Hank was careful not to appear too eager, or to be in too much of a hurry.

"Yeah, but them brokers don't git here afore 'bout nine or ten in the mornin'. You boys will just have to see Barney."

The two cowboy cousins decided they would head over to the registrar's office and then return to question the one named Barney. They got a good description of Getwood from the deputy clerk, but he was hesitant to agree to any deposition they may want.

"My description fits exactly with the man you described to me," the clerk did admit, "but that wasn't the name he gave or the name on our record sheet."

"What did you say that name was?"

"Woods," the man replied, to Hank.

"Thomas Woods, and here's his signature for our record application."

"Sure 'pears to me it's Getwood's writing," Cliff said, "though, I ain't seen him write much." "I never was sure he *could* write," said Hank.

By the time the cowboys returned to the stock pens, Taggart was gone somewhere, and they met Barney.

"Yup, Tag told me you was out here 'bout sun-up. He said you was lookin' fer a feller name of Get-work, or sumpthin'."

"Getwood . . . Getwood Hall. But we have reason to believe he's usin' the name of Woods, Thomas Woods."

"Yeah, I know that sumbitch, he's a hard-head. Taggart knows him, too. Surprised he didn't tell you."

"We didn't mention the name to your friend. We didn't know he was using it until we saw the registration clerk."

"Well, you're too late, his shipment never did show up, and he left outta here, mad as a wet rattlesnake."

* * *

Clifton and Hank walked over to the livery where Big Jake met them with both of their horses fed and well rested. Their decision was to ride back to their ranch after they told Jake all that they knew about the Piaute raid and the Jenson ranch tragedy.

"Diss man you des-kribe, you haff cum to try und locate, vas he riding a doppleed-grey gelding? Und mit froze-off ears on der sorrel dot he had too, ja?"

"Ja, I mean, yes," replied Hank.

"Vell, boise, he vas here, bot now iss not. He shtill owes me money, und he say he vould be beck, ja."

"That means he'll likely show-up for another shipment of stolen cattle," said Hank to Clifton.

"Except we don't know exactly when that will be, and with this mess with those Indians now, and the funeral for Daddy, I figure we should get back to the ranch right quick. We can always look again, in a couple of days."

"You're right, Cliff, we should get started as soon's we can. I want to cross that bad stretch of land before it gets too dark. So long, Dutch. We'll be back with our county sheriff soon and he'll want to talk with your marshal."

"Let's ride to the general store, Cliff, I think we should get some extra cartridges."

"Yeah, good idea. Adios, Jake."

There were no signs of any Indians on the trails Hank and Clifton took to home. They arrived at their corals just after sun-up, and rubbed down their tired horses. They both could hardly wait to see the women they adored.

Smiley Black-Wolf, one of the wagon hands, came in earlier that week from the range, to keep up with the chores. Smiley must have just milked the Guernsey, and fed the yard stock, before he left for the range work that day. The evidence was clear, as Clifton whistled at a cow-boy heading out the west pasture gate. Smiley waved back.

"See ya in a couple hours, Cliff," Hank said as he made his way to his cabin.

"Aren't you coming over for breakfast?" Cliff replied, as he chuckled at his lucky cousin. "What'll I tell ma and Mary Anne?"

"You'll think of somethin'," he said, while stepping on the porch to wash himself.

Clifton noticed the lamps were on in the main house before he entered, and saw a light at the rear of Hank's cabin. By the time Cliff started inside, he saw the light in Abbey and Hank's bedroom fade out.

"It's just delightful to awaken with a smile," she said to her handsome cowboy, "after a few days of concern for your return -I th . . ." Abbey squealed with delight.

"I guess I really should say hello to my Aunt Lucy," Hank kidded Abbey, while he was removing his boots at the side of the bed.

Abbey threw back the coverlet and quickly left her warmed side of the bed. She threw her arms around her husband's neck and shoulders, and forced him backward on the bed. "Your Aunt Lucy will just have to take her turn to see you, big guy. Right now, you are all mine."

Abbey kissed him fiercely and often, while he continued to divest himself of the balance of his cowboy clothes, including his hat.

"Sweetheart," he said, "I know it's been a few days, but I never knew how much I missed your warm and beautiful . . .sense of humor!"

"I can't let you talk, you just keep babbling, and I need your full concentration," Abbey replied, as she whacked him on his tight rear.

Their lips met again, this time with the full passions they both felt, and a softness of fondling ensued, as they caressed each other in love's embrace.

The two young people were deeply in love with one another, and the respect that Hank afforded Abbey always was paramount in her mind. She adored her tall cowboy, and emulated his open and positive approach to living life to its fullest.

Abbey's thoughts of sometime bearing a child with Hank, continued to haunt her, especially during their intimate embraces, but somehow she never spoke her mind aloud to her husband. There'd be lots of time later.

Mary Anne was almost finished feeding Cody when she heard Clifton greeting his mother from the parlor, next to the living room.

He hurried into the kitchen. Mary Anne arose from her seat next to the box cradle where the baby was being fed, and she reached out to lovingly embrace Clifton.

He kissed her, long and deep, while he lifted her svelte body off the floor and held her, oh, so tenderly.

"I'm sure glad glad to be back to you, darlin'. I didn't realize just how much I missed those pretty eyes and lovin' kisses."

"Oh, Cliff," Mary Anne cooed. "I've been counting the hours - you're practically all I've been thinking of since you asked me to marry you. I'm the luckiest gal in all this world . . .and just look at this little guy. When I do, I see you over and over again. He's so sweet, he's just like his da . . ."

"You're so beautiful, Mary Anne, even more each time I see you," he interrupted. "Hi, Cody, this is your Dad, and you're going to see a lot more of me, fella, and your new mom, too."

Cliff had his son in his own arms now, and was talking to him as he walked in the parlor where Aunt Lucy took the boy.

"I'm so glad you're home Clifton . . . and where's Hank, anyway?"

CHAPTER TWENTY TWO

A JAIL BREAK . . . THEN, AN AMBUSH

The cover of darkness afforded the nefarious group of bumbling outlaws a thin blanket of sorts under which they felt safe.

"You shore this is the right thang to do, jes slip into town thisaway and rush the jail, Boyle?"

"Shaddup, Lefty," Get said. "Ren Morgan's kin to you, ain't he? Anyways, we are gonna need him when we round up more beeves - and by God, this time we're gonna get it right, see?"

"Cookie, you ride around the backside of the sheriff's office and tie-up in the alley back there. Me and Palmer'll jes ride quietly down the center of town, and tie our horses at the hitch rail at the saloon. There should be several horses there, so we'll pick out a good-un fer when we bust out ol' Ren."

"Whacha want me to do, boss?"

"Wal, Lefty, It's up to you o ride up to the front and act natchural, in case there's anyone else 'ceptin the deputy on duty. If you see anybody else, just whistle 'Dixie'. Palmer and me will ride on to the alley where Cookie is."

"You want me to bust in that back door, don'tcha, Boyle. I kin do that, and then git the cell keys."

Myles Cooke was somewhat experienced in what job he had. He helped break a man out of jail four years ago, in Texas, and they all got away with no shots fired.

Cookie broke in the back door, stole the keys off a peg and unlocked the cell. He planned to enact this caper the same way. He needed Lefty to come up to the front door and inquire about something that would occupy the deputy or whomever was on duty.

When Cooke dismounted and slipped over to the back door of the sheriff's office, he tripped and nearly fell over a form all curled up at the end of the four-step porch.

"S'all right, Deputy, I'm willin' to be pee-saa-bill an' just go toooma-bunk." It was a sodden and sullen Rufus Higgenbotham, who had once more stupefied himself, awaiting Deputy Peabody's presence to escort him to his 'suite'.

"Damn town drunk," Myles muttered, while he knocked Rufus on his head with his pistol butt, and left him asleep in a heap where he first found him.

The ruckus woke up Ren Morgan, who stood on his bunk to see out the small cell window, adjacent to the back stairway, even in the dark.

* * *

Deputy Peabody was awakened by the rapping on the front door from Lefty.

"G'way, Rufus," the deputy mistakenly shouted, "I'm in no mood to mess with you this time of night. Go home, ya hear? If you're out there in the morning I'll have to arrest you again for disturbin' our peace."

Lefty kept on knocking until Peabody finally got up to get the door.

Just as the deputy was opening the front, he heard the commotion at the back door, and it diverted his attention enough that Lefty slipped inside and held his gun to Peabody's neck.

"Easy does it, Deputy," the kerchief covered face of Lefty spoke. "I got your gun now, and I'm fixin' to cover yer eyes with this -here bandanna. No need for you to see any more'n you already has."

Cookie was inside now, and gathering the keys to open the cell Ren was in. Lefty tied Peabody's hands and put him in Morgan's cell.

The three outlaws quickly exited the back door into the blackness of the alley, and past the fallen body of the knocked-out, drunken Rufus Higgenbotham.

Cookie walked to where his horse was tied and mounted, while Ren and Lefty went up the alley to the front of the building. At the same time, Getwood and Frank Palmer rode back across the street from where they had stolen a 'flea-bitten' grey horse, with a 'BOX K' brand on it's left flank.

"I ist newp you boyths' 'ud come," lisped Ren, "I ist neber knewf when . . ."

"Shaddap, and ride, Morgan," Getwood hollered, "we've gotta get away 'fore them boys come outta that saloon . . . S'matter with your mouth, Morgan?"

"What's your plan, boss?" Palmer asked.

"We're a-headin' for Carson City."

* * *

High among the boulders, across from Caliénte Creek, where it wound its way to the Blue Sand mountain range, the two, Piaute scouts could see most of the surrounding land. The cool, clear-blue Nevada sky began to welcome the early dawn.

Shik-ta-yå and *Ish-tåå* finished eating their spit-skewered, desert rabbit, dug a shallow hole and packed all the remaining fire residue and uneaten bones under the dirt.

When they left this post there would be no evidence of them or anyone being there.

"*Woéak-ti, gui-jima, hø,*" one said.

"Quickly, you see all five white-eyes now water pony at stream, look, *Ish-tåå,* now!"

"*Ugnh,* I see," replied the warrior.

The scouting mission was completed when the two Indians contacted the main warrior band, camped several miles from the boulders, and nearer the creek source.

It was likely that El Ladrøn would send only about fifteen of his braves to overtake this group. They would be led by *Shik-ta-yå* and *Ish-tåå,* rewarding them for their keen perception. These two scouts were mounted on two handsome Tobiano-Pintos, almost identical in color and size. Their horses were painted with four red stripes across each of their two front legs, denoting battles they rode in, and each with the sign of the bear on their flank, painted in black. The bear showed to which clan the two braves belonged.

* * *

Myles Cooke was riding in front and Getwood and Ren were riding side by side, and behind him. Lefty and Frank Palmer were also riding abreast in the rear, as they all rode from the creek when they were finished watering their horses.

"I'll be glad to get to Walker Lake," said Myles, "I have some unfinished business there. You a-comin' with me, Frank?"

"I guess. You want us to meet at the Dixon cabin Saturday, that right, Boyle?"

"Yeah, we're gonna leave you up here at the crossing, 'cause we're ridin' into Hawthorne. I want to get me some new duds, and a haircut and a shave . . and another saddle blanket. This one's a mess. Guess we can afford to buy alot o' things we want now, since we got ourselves some walkin' around money."

"We'll all meet at the cabin Saturday morning. Frank, you and Myles better bring some more grub when you come. I been thinkin' on some new plans," Getwood announced to all.

* * *

Myles' horse was struck in the eye with the first arrow, and the second one buried itself deep into the chest and on to the heart, dropping the horse immediately.

Myles caught a long arrow in his thigh, and another directly in his throat. He clutched his neck, but could not scream, and fell to the dirt, dying in agony, in his own pool of blood.

No one suspected the ambush, but it was a perfect spot to enable the band of warriors enough cover on one side, and an open area on the other. The hidden Indians were causing all the current damage, and were whooping and screaming, and rushing the outlaws, while shooting their arrows.

They displayed an outstanding show of riding skill, much like the plains Indians of the Comanche nation. The rope that girthed their ponies was used to place one foot and leg over its back, while leaning from the off side, under the animal's neck, to shoot their arrows from the short bow.

The second wave of arrows were dispersed by the balance of the warriors that rode out of the gully, and approached from behind the doomed, outnumbered outlaws.

By this time, Getwood and Palmer had their carbines out of the scabbards and were firing randomly, at the red marauders.

The second group of Piautes was led by *Shik-ta-yå,* screaming loudly.

Ren Morgan rode his flea-bit grey directly in front of a tall brave, who was wielding his feather adorned, war-lance. Morgan dodged the warriors thrust, and then grabbed the arm of the renegade.

The two fell to the ground and Ren leaped on his foe, grabbed the lance, and thrust it deep into his neck and shoulder, pinning him down.

Life left the brave with a strangulated gurgle, as blood erupted from his throat and turned the grainy earth from a golden brown to a brilliant crimson.

The very second that Lefty Barker saw the horse that Myles was riding hit by the arrow, he wheeled his pony and headed as fast as the horse could run, down an embankment. He momentarily escaped the view from the second group of Indians that attacked from the rear.

Miraculously, no one saw Lefty after he managed to escape the wild frenzy, in that first, loud moment.

Lefty kept after his game little Pinto pony, to continue to run as fast as he knew how. That horse had a heart as big as he was, and he laid his ears back, and stuck his neck forward, and gave his rider the very best he had. He ran for about two miles with Lefty spurring him and urging him to carry him faster and faster, over some rocky terrain and through some stag-horn cholla cactus,that tore at the hide of the little horse and its rider.

Finally, the horse quit running, and no amount of whipping, and spurring could force him to continue. Lefty slapped him in frustration, and cursed him, but his gallant little pony, just then, rolled over, took his last long gasp of air, and sadly died.

Lefty, of course, was furious, but he was just too dumb to blame himself. He gathered what he could of his gear, and constantly looking over his shoulder for any sign of an enemy, started out afoot for Fort Carson.

He took his saddle bags with some food and all the money, and his canteen and rifle and six-gun, but he had to leave his saddle. There was no way he could get if off the dead horse, unless he cut it. He finally figured out he wouldn't want to carry it, anyway.

* * *

Frank Palmer shot a Piaute brave off his horse and was about to level is Sharps at another, when one Indian leaped from his own horse on to the back of Frank's, landing behind his saddle. That force unseated Frank Palmer, and he and the Piaute fell to the ground. Two Indians jumped on him and held him down. They didn't kill him then, because *Ish-tåå* motioned them not to.

Ren Morgan regained his feet and was trying to catch his loose horse, when he took two arrows in his back that drove him forward to the desert floor.

One small Indian lad screamed a yell and drove his lance clear through the chest of Morgan, tearing his stomach out. The lad quickly grabbed the grey horse, and with a scream of triumph, claimed it as his very own.

Getwood was desperately fighting with a huge red man, while they both were on the ground. As they rolled over, Getwood managed to grab the long knife from the Piaute, and plunge it directly into his midsection. He grasped the knife with both hands, and with all the strength he had left, twisted and thrust upward, splitting the sternum. A quick rip of pressure and this one joined another of his brothers in a gristly death.

As Getwood arose, two braves, one on each side of him, grabbed his arms and lifted him between them and placed him down hard in front of the rest.

They'd all now formed a circle around their captors. Getwood saw that Myles was dead, and Ren, too. He and Palmer were alive, but where was Lefty?

CHAPTER TWENTY THREE

A WHIMSICAL PROPOSAL . . . AND CAPTIVES PONDER THEIR FATE

Another majestic, western dawn was greeted by an early rising, yellow-ochre sun at the cow ranch, where Aunt Lucy was busy preparing one of her famous ranch breakfasts.

This was the day the women arranged with the undertaker, Caleb, and Preacher Tom Dalton, to hold a funeral service and an interment at the church plot in Walker Lake.

It was scheduled for about noon, and that would allow enough time for all to return to the ranch for evening chores.

After breakfast, Clifton motioned to Mary Anne to step out the back door with him. She quickly followed him over to the spring house.

"Cliff, what're you grinning about?"

"I've thought of a terrific idea. What would you say to us gettin' the preacher to marry us after the funeral service today?"

"W-wh . . .I-I guess it would be . . .why, sure. Okay, I mean, of course. If you think your mother . . .I-I mean, oh, yes, yes, darlin', that's just wonderful."

"We'll take the buggy and Jamima back to the livery, and tie our two saddle horses to the back of the rig, for our ride back home. Hank and Abbey can take Mother and Cody back home with them, in the spring-board."

"You can bet Hank will sure take care of the chores, 'til we get back the next evening; besides, Smiley'll most likely stop to help him."

"The . . . next evening? . . . Tomorrow?" Mary Anne said, puzzled.

"Sure. We can spend the night at the hotel, and catch up on . . . our sleep," Cliff answered, with a grin. "It will do us right. Heck, we might just even stay an extra day. That'll give you a good chance to visit with Mazie and Edna, and some of your other friends."

Cliff continued, "I guess your old boss has been wondering what's become of you, anyway. You can collect your back wages and inform him of your decision to become a settled-down, old married woman."

Mary Anne playfully pushed Cliff with both hands to his chest, and reached her toe behind his boot to trip him, and shoved him backward into the dirt.

The ground at the side of the spring house wasn't exactly a soft feather bed, but Clifton reached up and grabbed both of Mary Anne's legs, locked them together, and then pulled her gently downward onto him.

They warmly kissed while they firmly embraced in each other's arms.

"Oh, sweetheart," Mary Anne breathlessly said, "do you really think this is the right time for us to marry, I mean . . . with your daddy's funeral, and all the nasty things happening with Getwood, and . . ."

"Of, course, and so will the family, you'll see. I'll explain it all. Now, let's get ourselves ready."

* * *

A warming sun finally found its way to the back of the alley, behind the Walker Lake jailhouse. and awakened Rufus from his all night sleep. The gash on the back of his head had clotted and closed, and given that he had a perpetual headache, he stood on his feet, none the worse for wear.

The back door was open and he made his way inside the jail. Deputy Peabody was aroused by the noise Rufus made, as he unlocked the cell door with the keys he had found.

"Untie me, Rufus," the deputy exclaimed, with a loud but muffled voice from under his bandanna.

"W-what happened, Deputy?" Rufus quizzed.

"Jail break, you idjut!" Peabody answered. "Go find the sheriff, Rufus, as quick as you can. He might be eatin' with his missus, to home, or he might be at the livery barn. Hurry."

The west bound stage was due in a short while and Sheriff Sager was at the livery stable overlooking the three teams of horses being readied for the switch with those arriving.

Deputy Peabody was hoping the Pinkerton man the sheriff wired was aboard. They were going to need some help to solve last nights breakout from the jail.

Peabody was sure the Pinkerton detective was bringing some information regarding the cattle rustlers, and now, he would find out about the jail break, and work on that, too.

Rufus met the sheriff coming to the jail. "Peabody's in j-jail, Sheriff. I-I mean he was in jail and now, I-I jes let him out."

Rufus was stammering as he tried to explain the jail break to the sheriff.

Jim Sager had been the sheriff in Mineral County for about four years, nine years after Nevada became a state, in 1864. He was impervious to, and stoic about the conversation Rufus was relating.

"Here's a dollar, Rufus, why don't you go get some breakfast and sober up? I can take care of matters at my own jail."

Rufus spoke not a word. He just grinned, pivoted, and made a bee-line for the saloon.

The sheriff last saw Peabody when they said their good-nights at the shift change last night, so he was stunned when he heard the wild story his deputy told him.

"I never seen the mans face," cried Pea. "He had it covered with a bandanna, and besides, he told me not to look around when he put the blindfold on me." The deputy was trying to explain his ineptness to the sheriff, who wondered just how many people were involved.

"I know there were at least three men in on it," said the deputy. "Morgan kept callin' one of 'em Lefty. And somebody must'a broke in the back door whilst I was see'n to the front."

"I thought it was ol' Rufus, drunk on the front porch and I was near 'bout ready to get him in when I heered this loud noise at the back door. I turned around to see, and that feller put the gun on me."

* * *

The small band of Piautes were depleted by the loss of two of their braves in the ambush. Sadly, they wrapped the bodies in blankets, and placed them on two ponies, and proceeded to take them along to their main camp site.

Frank Palmer and Getwood Hall, both whose hands were tethered, were also put on their horses and forced to ride with the rest.

"*Hü,*" cried *Ish-tåå,* when the band rode in and reported to El Ladrøn. "We are sad, but proud to bring two gallant brothers back to council. They give up life to afford us memory of their brave acts against enemy. We bring two more white-eyes for council's wishes."

"*Hü, El Ladrøn.*" *Shik-ta-yå* spoke. "Our search to capture all five enemy was spoiled by loss of three of them. One was struck down by *Ahîka,* the cub. He now sits before you on captured pony from enemy."

"Another," he went on, "the first to fall, I claim. I shoot both horse and rider, and I shake killing gourd over body."

"Where is third?" The chief asked. "Why you not tell of his death?"

"We bring two with us, *Jéfe*," said *Shik-ta-yå*. "Sadly, we can not tell of third. Yellow Deer saw him riding a spotted horse, and while he was kept busy in our brave fight with enemy, lost sight of both horse and rider. No one see 'um."

"What're they gonna do with us, Boyle?" Frank Palmer questioned Getwood. "Kill us?"

Lefty Barker wished he was a little boy again, back on the Kansas wheat farm his mother and father homesteaded. He wished his bird-dog puppy was still at his side, and he wished that 'Muddy', the brown mule was at the rails where he could shinny-up the harness and grab a hame-strap, so he could ride him from the creek to the barn, at home.

It was mid afternoon, and Lefty had long since finished the water in his canteen. He had some jerky and a can of peaches in his saddle bags, along with about eight hundred dollars. He slowly emerged from his wishful thinking trance, and sat down where he was, in the middle of nowhere, on his way to Fort Carson.

* * *

One of the Army scouts spotted the fire that Lefty carelessly built on the desert floor, and rode back to report to the main column.

"I don't think the fire belongs to any Shoshone or any Piaute, Captain," the scout reported. "can't figure who would light a fire in the middle of the open like that, with all the trouble from 'The Robber' and his band of cut-throats. I think it's maybe only one man, sir."

"Sergeant, take one squad from B company and follow the scout to investigate. Whoever it is, I wish to speak with them."

Sergeant Muldoon, and the eight man squad, immediately wheeled, and two by two, rode out with the scout to where the fire was warming a disoriented and frightened Lefty Barker.

"How many were there?" The captain kept on asking Lefty. "And just exactly where did you first encounter them? What's happened with your horse, mister?"

Lefty was at a loss to explain all he was asked in any detail. He remained as vague as he could, and was as careful he did not disclose any information that could incriminate him with the jail break with which he was involved.

A detail of three men, one corporal and two troopers, were assigned to take Lefty to the fort. The mule he rode was one of ten braces accompanying the soldiers. He was to be turned over to the Provost Marshal's office for further interrogation, after the eight hundred dollars was found in his saddle bags. He tied his saddle bag on the back of the Army saddle that was held firm with the help of a britchen.

"Want some peaches?" he stupidly said to the corporal.

"Guide-on to the front," barked the officer, as the regiment prepared to move onward in their search for the Indians, toward the Wassuk mountain range.

"We will bivouac today at 1800 hours, Sergeant, Scouts out," he commanded. "Column of fours- foaar'd, ho-o."

The column moved over the land all dotted with the white sage and greasewood, prevalent to this area in the northwest-central part of Nevada,

There were a few mesquite trees that were small because they craved water, and up the slopes, grew the sparse piñon pine.

CHAPTER TWENTY FOUR

THE RAID

The Hall's reined up in front of Ruby's cafe, one of several places in town that served meals daily, including the hotel. Hank tied the team and the springboard to the hitching rail, while Abbey and Aunt Lucy carefully unloaded the baby and a few of the child's dry goods.

"We'll be back soon," said Clifton, as he and Mary Anne rode toward the livery to return the black mare and the buggy.

While he and Mary Anne were riding their saddle horses up the street to Ruby's, they spied the Reverend Dalton crossing the street.

"Hold on, Preacher," Cliff excitedly spoke. He stepped down from Dobie, handed a rein to Mary Anne, and took the preacher's arm to guide him to where they both were.

"Would you be willing to perform a marriage ceremony later today, after Daddy's funeral?" Cliff implored the preacher.

"Of course I would. Is it someone I might know? Preacher Dalton replied.

"Mary Anne and me," a bashful voice answered him.

* * *

"You're invited to a wedding, Jim," Cliff said to the sheriff, whom he'd just seen, after an arrangement with the preacher was settled.

"Don't allow that I've got the time to spare. Who is it that you're a-talkin' a. . . ?"

"I've asked Mary Anne to hitch up double with me, Jim, and we're getting married later today, after Clyde's funeral."

"Well, son, I'm proud for ya, and Mary Anne's a sweetheart who's just right for you, but I have to tell you that I flat forgot about Caleb tellin' me that Clyde's funeral was today, then you tell me of a big wedding after . . ."

"Naw, not a big wedding, Jim. We just decided to marry-up while we all were together in town, and a few of Mary Anne's old girl friends are coming, and Hank'll stand up for me, and it . . ."

"Cliff, there's something that you should know. The jail was busted into yesterday in the early morning or during the night, and whoever was involved took our prisoner, Ren Morgan, with them. 'Course, you know who I suspect!"

"Hank and Abbey are over to Ruby's, along with Ma and my baby boy. I'll tell Hank, but I'd appreciate it if you wouldn't mention any of this to my mother."

"Cliff, my deputy and a few of the boys are gettin' ready to form a posse. I know Soapy and Martin Reyés, and maybe ol' Harry Carter's comin'. We could all wait until after the funeral and your wedding, afore we ride out."

"Been a pleasure seen' you, Mary Anne, I wish you both all the very best."

* * *

The area was secured by the Army troops at the western most approach to the Wassuk mountains, on high ground suitable for the night's bivouac. The mess tents were set up for the officers and the non-commissioned officers, while the cavalry men ate by their horses at the picket lines.

After mess, the bugler sounded officers call, later he sounded tattoo, and finally, at 2100 hours, he sounded taps.

* * *

At least twenty warriors, including some of the best horsemen of the red men, surrounded the horse herd at the south end of the Army camp. As soon as a skirmish was started at the north-west corner from the arroyo toward the foothills of the Wasasuks, the horse stealers started their raid.

"Hey, Collins, you awake? You hear that? It sounds like gun fire." And trooper Wilkes shook his pal awake.

"Can't be Injuns, can it? I thought those red sticks didn't have no rifles."

"It's probably our sentries," Wilkes yelled. "Get up." The gunfire was becoming much more intense, and now the screaming and yelling from the Piautes, who were rushing the encampment from the foothills became individual, blood-curdling war whoops.

Unlike regimented charges from the soldiers, the Indians were acting each on their own as they rode, wave after wave, throughout the even spaced pup tents of the troopers, lances drawn, arrows flying.

Most of the platoons were trying to form in front of their tents. Sergeants and corporals were screaming orders to the men.

The Calvary soldiers were scrambled with abandonment to saddle their individual mounts. it was both difficult and frustrating because, by this time the Indians that were raiding the horse herd, cut the picket lines, and with their yelling and waving blankets in the air, managed to spook the horses. Much later, the soldiers were able to re-group and capture back most of the horses.

According to regulations, the rifles were stacked in front of the tents. They were leaning against one another in groups to form a tripod. The first wave of the Indian riders knocked over most of the arms and their horses stepped on them, and then scattered the remainder.

The regimental bugler was cut down early in the fray, by at least ten arrows, as soon as he blew boots-and-saddles.

Trooper Wilkes stepped from his tent and into the path of an oncoming mounted warrior, who split his skull in two pieces. Collins was right behind him and became sick and vomited before he could find his rifle.

Corporal Cooper and trooper Madison found their weapons and were making a back to back stand in the cover of some iron wood trees. The Lieutenant was near by and he was firing his sidearm. At his feet lay two dead Piautes. After the initial attack by the Indians riding in from the north-west side subsided, and the brave stand of A Company and H Company excelled, the tempo of the battle slowed considerably.

The fire power the soldiers employed was now beginning to become effective, as more and more troopers were able to fire their repeating rifles. The men in A Company were especially trenchant due mostly because they were encamped about fifty yards from the rest. H Company, in charge of the ordinance, issued ammunition to the rest of the companies, then joined in the battle.

The lances and war clubs the Indians had were only useful in close-up, hand-to-hand combat, and most of them spent their arrows in the first two assaults.

It was not yet ten o'clock at night, and the Piaute raiders were disbursing very quickly. Only a few of the bravest warriors attempted to retrieve some of their wounded.

The balance were scattering, and losing themselves in the darkness. Trooper Collins, abashed, put to use the skill he'd been perfect-ing, when he found a bugle and blew assembly, then officers call.

Less than seventy of well over one hundred Piaute Indian raiders met the following morning, at a pre-destined place of gathering, where a guard group assigned to watch their prisoners, set a camp. They were about twenty five miles from where the raid took place at the foot of the Wassuk mountains.

Many braves were nursing severe injuries from falls from their horses, as well as injuries from sword and rifle bullets.

The dejected band, painfully and slowly began their journey to the far hills, where a village housed women and children.

El Ladrøn and *Arbøl Colorådo* led the defeated Indian assembly to their homeland. At the bend in the river they were to cross, two scouts on lathered ponies, loped toward them and told of the impending approach of a long column of pony-soldiers. Another half mile behind them were wagons carrying three companies of infantry.

One of the scouts, who had slashed his hair in grief, told his *Jéfe* that he counted over three times one hundred soldiers, and the mules were pulling great 'iron kettle' guns up on wagon wheels.

The regiment was in marching force.

The Indians stopped their march, and were told by *El Ladrøn* to stick their lances in front of them in the ground, throw down their bows and clubs, and form in two lines behind each other. The prisoners were placed in front of the lines, mounted and still tied. The two chiefs rode to the very front to face the soldier column that was now forming a skirmish line, and approaching less than 500 yards away.

"Troop, hal-l-lt! Guide-on, front and center. Lieutenant, Sergeant Muldoon! You will approach the red men with me. H Company, flank right. F Company, to the left. Ho-o! -Bugler, stand by."

Slowly and deliberately the captain and his troopers rode to within ten yards of the two chiefs.

"Hü, etå," said *El Ladrøn.* We no more will fight. Our brave warriors are hurt and sick, and pony herd is tired and few. Our bellies are empty. We need food and blankets for children. We ask you not take land where we hunt and make camps . . . we no

more fight pony-sol-dier from your Fort 'Kar-sun'. We offer you five men who fought us, and are now for your care. You take,"

The captain was astonished to discover the men were unhurt. Among them was Ezra Jenson, Frank Palmer and Getwood Hall.

* * *

The regiment was intercepted on the way back to Fort Carson the following day, before noon. A posse consisting of the men from Walker Lake came upon the Army encampment at their noon repast.

"Halt. Advance and be recognized," the sentry called out to the posse. After identities were sorted the group rode to see the captain.

Martin Reyés held the horses when the sheriff approached the captain's tent. The sheriff saw Getwood Hall, seated cross-legged, eating a meal with several line officers nearby. Across from him sat Frank Palmer and another civilian.

"Greetings, Sheriff," spoke the captain. "You men will join us for some bread pudding and coffee? What's your posse doing here, this far from your jurisdiction?"

Getwood whirled around, and started to rise, when he saw who the captain was addressing.

"I have a state issued warrant for the arrest of this very man," Sheriff Sager said, as he drew his side arm and leveled it at Getwood.

Frank Palmer immediately rose and attempted to grab a pistol from the soldier on his left.

"Put your hands on top o'yore haid, mister," came word from the deputy, who was quickly at his side.

"What're you doing with these civilians, Captain? We've been after these two for quite some time," the sheriff questioned.

It only took a short while for the sheriff to explain the entire situation to the Army officers, and to persuade them the posse should return to Walker Lake with both men.

The Pinkerton detective was riding with the posse, and he identified Palmer. Harry Carter had to be restrained to keep from punching Getwood Hall.

"I can't wait to see what Cliff and Hank have in mind for you. As for me, I'm for hangin' cow thieves, and you're one," Harry said.

Ezra Jenson and the two cowboys that worked for him were fed and comforted and free to go their way; however, the three decided they'd go to Fort Carson after Lieutenant McVey disclosed the fate of Ezra's wife and his ranch. He was the reconnaissance officer that investigated the fire.

Sam and Charlie, Ezra's cowhands, decided they'd help Ezra rebuild his homestead and help with his strayed cattle, later.

With the Indian uprising settled, for now, and the men who'd been taken in as prisoners cared for, the posse left the Army encampment early afternoon for their trip to Walker Lake. Getwood Hall and Frank Palmer would be held in the Walker Lake jail to await their fate.

The Army regiment arrived at the fort about the same time the posse arrived in Walker Lake.

CHAPTER TWENTY FIVE

AWAITING EXTRADITION

Hank was driving the springboard wagon back to the Circle Diamond cow ranch after the days events were finished.

Aunt Lucy seemed resigned to her years at the ranch without her beloved Clyde. She was also looking forward to the upbringing of her stout little grandson, and to Mary Anne, and her son's married life, all as one big, happy family.

Her thoughts drifted away toward a disturbed Getwood and what fate may lie in store for him. The baby was fast asleep in his grandmother's arms, rocked into peacefulness by the steady clop, clop as the team slow-trotted along the rocky road to the home ranch.

"I'm just thrilled for Mary Anne and Cliff, aren't you, sweetheart?" Abbey snuggled closer to Hank in the front seat, when she asked the question.

"You bet, and I know Aunt Lucy is thrilled, too. But, uppermost in my mind now is the situation with Get. We've simply got to find him and make him pay for his crooked ways. We catch him, he's goin' back to the Carson City pen, and they may just hang him. Cliff and I'll see the sheriff in a couple of days, after Cliff's totally rested."

Hank chuckled, as he pursed to the fine sorrel team hitched to the wagon.

Several dog-coyotes were serenading their mates from a nearby mesa, as Hank and his family were nearing the outskirts of their Circle Diamond cow ranch.

"It's good to be home again," Abbey spoke, when she lithely jumped down from the spring wagon, and took Cody from his grandmother's arms. Hank helped his Aunt Lucy with her packages, for it seemed no one ever went to town without bringing back a supply of needed ranch reserves.

Hank unhitched the team, then watered and fed them well, before he completed some other evening chores, including milking the little pet Guernsey cow.

Hank set the milk pail down, and he released the cow from the stanchion, and was heading toward the spring house when he stopped abruptly. "Well, well," he exclaimed. This is a surprise . What're you a-doin' out here?"

She had her blouse unbuttoned, and the top of her tight jeans opened at the belt. She reached out with both arms and unfolded herself into his chest.

"Amazing," he said. "I-I didn't th . . ." She never let him finish. She kissed him so ardently and with such fury, that she began to hold nothing back.

"You might've caught me off guard, but it's not like I'm ever totally amazed at your actions." He gently lifted her heated body in his arms, turned, and carefully laid her down in the freshly bedded stall in the back side of the dimly lit stable.

"You know, I believe I can still hear those coyotes a-howlin'," he whispered. "Or maybe it's just a wild reaction I have to this wonderful happening. I must say, darlin', this does help the cravin' I constantly have for you."

"Kiss me, oh, kiss me Hank," Abbey gasped. "I can't wait another minute. Make love with me, hurry. Oh, please," she urged.

He quickly and quietly gratified her patent, burning passions, and totally appeased his own inner-self with a compassionate approach to his only true love. And so, the cowboy and his lady faded into a comfortable slumber.

The daylight was late for Hank's arising, and he covered Abbey with another of the clean, wool horse blankets from the adjoining tack-room. He started the morning chores, and laughed aloud, allowing his cute, sleepy wife to tend to her own daytime duties. Cody would waken soon, and Aunt Lucy would start the big ranch breakfast.

The Nevada morning sky was a pied mixture of red and gray, and the cumulus clouds that hovered were suddenly lower, and racing with the wind. The rain came across the land from out of the northwest, and it settled down at the Circle Diamond. For a rancher, it was truly a welcome sight. The arid territory soaked up the water just as quickly as it fell, until finally, with no place for it to go, started to collect.

Aunt Lucy gave her grandson his breakfast, and waited for Abbey and Hank to join her in the kitchen.

* * *

A letter arrived for Lefty Barker in Walker Lake. Billy Howe took it, along with the rest of the undelivered mail, to the county attorney's office on the second floor of the bank. Abe Klein placed it in a box with the other mail he wished to sort, to try to find the addressee.

Billy also told Mister Klein about the posse and the two captured crooks they put in the jail house, last night.

When the federal circuit rider came through Walker Lake he informed the solicitor that the Army released a list of some liberated settlers and some ranchers they held at the fort after the Indian raids.

The list included the names of Ezra Jenson, Lefty Barker and Joseph August, among others. There was also a letter that was addressed to a Mrs. Lucille Hall at the C.D. Ranch, with a smudged return name. It was from Carson City, and it was left with the hotel clerk to give to Clifton Hall.

Word spreads fast in a small town, and Billy Howe was quick to relate to each clerk for whom he did chores, the names of the men who were held in the town jail.

Clifton and his new bride, Mary Anne, were in the hotel dining room when Abner and Clara Walsh, who owned the mercantile, entered in.

"Well, hello, Clifton," Abner greeted him . . and - ohm, oh, howdy, uh, uh, Mary Anne, ain't it? This here's the missus, uh, Clarabelle."

"Howdy, Abner. Mrs. Walsh, may I present my new wife, Mary Anne. I believe you know Mary Anne, right, Abner?" Cliff strained to keep from laughing, as he saw the reaction from Clarabelle Walsh, one of the town's busiest busybodies.

"Won't you join us for some supper?" Mary Anne said to the couple, knowing full-well their answer.

"Oh, we'd be right honored to help celebrate the grand occasion of . . . "

"No. Uh, I-uh, mean - I'm sorry," interrupted Abner's wife, tersely. "We -uh, have a shipment of goods that just arrived that must be placed in stock. We simply cannot spare the time. We only stopped to see about some other bus . . ."

"Sorry, Cliff, Mary Anne. I'll see you soon." Abner bumped the table when his wife grabbed his arm to lead him from the dining room. "Cliff," whispered Abner, as he passed. "The sheriff's got Getwood in the jail house an- at's all I know."

"Close call, sweetheart," Mary Anne chuckled. "We almost lost the privacy we . . . what's wrong?" Why the sullenness, Cliff?" she clutched his arm and asked; "What did Abner whisper to you just then, when he passed the table?"

"I'll tell you, it's something I was hoping for. Now how 'bout some more wine?"

* * *

The rain did the right thing by soaking the land and adding to the water table for all the wells in Mineral County.

The sunshine that soon followed, suggested to the wild flowers they should make their appearance known.

The fragrant aromas of mesquite, and the greasewood, as well as juniper, fresh from a rainstorm and warmed by the sun, wafted into town and added to the charms of Walker Lake.

* * *

After his breakfast at Ruby's cafe, Deputy Peabody drifted back and forth down the main street, inspecting the various business houses and other establishments, on his way to the livery stables.

"Mornin', Pea," Hiram McCoy nodded. "Come have a look-see at what happened while you was a-chasin' them outlaws. About two weeks ago, or so, I come to warter all the animals, an' that there second stall, way in the back, I seen whut you're a-lookin' at now."

It was breakfast time for seven of the cutest, brown and black and white puppies, that had ever been whelped in a long while.

"Why, that's your good dog, Molly, ain't it?" Pea winked at Hiram, and said, "she must'a got lucky with one that looks jes like her, 'cordin' to all the markings' on them pups. Whut boy dog has been around, Hiram?"

I'm purty shore it was that cow dog of Halls', them pups is all hunnert-per-cent same breed," Hiram stated. "You remember ol' Ranger, don'tcha, Deputy?"

"Shore do. I 'member that dog that follered ol' Clyde near 'bot ever'whar. Hank told me that dog got killed by a big-ol' badger. Reckon you'd let them Hall boys have one of them puppies when they'us weaned?"

"You betcha," Hiram replied. "I know Clifton and Mary Anne's spendin' a day or two in town, since they got hitched-up.

I b'leve I'll find 'em and show 'em this here litter of pups. They can pick out any one they'd like."

When Deputy Peabody returned to the office at the jail, the Pinkerton man was with the sheriff and they were questioning the prisoners, one at a time.

"Guess you know by now, Getwood, we got all the information we need to hold you for the United States marshal. He'll be here day after tomorrow. It looks as though you and Palmer here, are goin' to the pen in Carson City. Sheriff Sager wanted to know also, where the rest of the stolen money from the mining company is. He wired the company, and they were sending over a mine detective to question Getwood. The sheriff questioned Palmer about it first.

"Who else helped you in the mining company caper, Palmer?" The Pinkerton detective already had copious notes on the deed. He wanted a statement from Palmer, however.

In the adjoining room, Sheriff Sager was with Getwood, questioning him about the rustling that had been gong on for a time.

"It is true, is it not, you formed a gang to help you? Who is your contact in Carson City?" Getwood thought he needed a lawyer.

Abe Klein, the attorney who was the solicitor, agreed to set in on the interrogation of the prisoners after the deputy went to his office to accompany him.

There was a detailed description of all the events that took place over the many months of trouble caused by Getwood Hall. Of course, he placed the blame on Lefty and on Ren Morgan, claiming it was Lefty's idea to rustle the stock.

Getwood said that Lefty had a cohort at the Carson City stock pens to divert any shipments of stolen beef, and he named Taggart.

Palmer was blaming the whole mining company payroll robbery on his pal, Cooke. He said he was only involved because the company refused him back wages he claimed they owed him. He finally told where the rest of the payroll money was hidden, when Abe Klein pledged his assistance, and asked for some trade-off if Palmer told where the rest of the money was.

Sheriff Sager was just as concerned about the uprising caused by those Piautes riding with *El Ladrøn,* and was comforted in the fact that the Army defeated the Indians, and returned to the fort. Jim Sager was not aware the Army had taken Lefty to the fort.

This time, it looked as if Getwood was in more trouble, because he violated his parole agreement by engaging in a felony. Cattle rustling was an offense that usually resulted in a hanging sentence.

Abe Klein suddenly decided he had a business meeting he could not miss over in Virginia City, and naturally, he quickly departed.

* * *

The delay of their morning rising cause no immediate concern for Mary Anne and Cliff. The cool breeze that flowed through the open window in their room at the Palace Hotel was refreshing and called for a closer reunion of their bodies.

Mary Anne was breathing heavily as she raised her arm to place it above Cliff's shoulder, and around his neck. "I-I uh, oh, I want to kiss you and - oh, I need your love, darlin', now . . .oh, now, now."

"This is a complete fulfillment of my dreams and desires. When I first saw you, Cliff, I was so envious of your beautiful Caroline, and I dared not say a word to allow you to think I felt that way. I merely admired you from afar, and I accepted my lot."

Cliff ardently replied," Your compassion and your composure during the months has reinforced all the good thoughts I always had for you. My love for you grows stronger and deeper each hour that we're together. I so look forward to our life with each other at the Circle Diamond. Oh, Mary Anne, sweetheart, I love you very, very much."

Her rapture conveyed her passions as she held him even tighter. She interrupted him with more of her heated lovemaking.

"You are delicious," he said, as together, they drifted back to sleep.

CHAPTER TWENTY SIX

GETTING ON WITH RANCH BUSINESS

It was a large bay horse, with a blaze face, that was causing Hank a lot of trouble. Smiley Black-Wolf came from the wagon crew to help with some ranch chores. He had the horse roped and well snubbed.

This five year old stallion was overdue for castration, and the two cowboys decided to enact this quick operation before the heat of the day befell them.

Each time Hank approached the stud, it would move forward, take some slack out of the snub rope, and rear-up on his hind legs to strike out at him. He finally roped the horse's hind feet and stretched him out on the dirt in the round horse corral.

Smiley put a long and large cotton rope around the bay at his shoulder, and Hank tied another on it's hind legs and then secured it through the shoulder rope. Since the horse was already down, he had to be held down by kneeling on his neck, firmly.

Hank was about to perform the cut, when the stallion jerked free from Smiley's grasp and regained it's feet, bellering and snorting. The horse kicked to free itself and managed to jump the rope, throwing the slack in it, spun around and wrapped Smiley around his waist, and was starting to drag him about the corral.

Hank reacted quickly and cut the rope between both the cowboy and the horse in time to prevent a worse fate. Performing all the tasks that are required to handle horses are sometimes precarious, but usually routine. In most cases the horse reacts to a situation out of fear.

These are prey animals, not predators, therefore, it's a natural instinct to evade what it considers a peril to itself. Hank was a good horse-breaker, and he knew some idiosyncrasies of the animal to watch for.

When he caught the horse, moments later, he began to gentle him down by quietly talking to him. The castration job would have to be postponed until a later time, so Hank placed the stud in the large pole corral next to the barn, and then turned all of his attention to Smiley, who now seemed to be none the worse for wear.

The two cowboys went to the south corral, where five of the remuda horses were being kept in order to put new shoes on them. In this semi-rocky land most of the 'usin' horses had to be shod every six to seven weeks. This chore was usually done by Hank, so he was pleased that Smiley was feeling well enough to help him.

Smiley was a stoic individual who was used to a life of working with horses. He was a full-blooded, Shivwit Indian, and a member of a tribe that is a sub-division of the Piaute nation. He was adopted long ago by an early Mormon pioneer family and taught the language and work ethic of the Christian white man.

He started to work for the Halls on the Circle Diamond cow ranch when Cliff and Hank were young boys.

The two finished the horse shoeing in about an hour and a half. Hank told Smiley that he would be needed more with the wagons and the range stock than here, at headquarters. "And besides, Cliff's due back soon, likely tomorrow, and the two of us can handle the chores, including the horse-breaking. Go ahead on back with the wagons, pard, and don't get caught-up in any more ropes."

Hank thought better after he said that, hoping it wouldn't upset the Indian's self-pride, and said he needed him this Saturday, sure.

Hank busied himself next by repairing the wind mill at the far end of the long corral. He needed to replace the sleeve that covered the shaft that did the pumping. He was secretly wishing that Cliff would come back earlier, and the two of them could pick up where they left off in their search for Getwood.

There were several pieces of tack that needed some repair work, especially on the large harness sets used on the draft horse team. Now was as good a time as any, he thought, and took down one of the heavy horse collars and head stalls, and began placing them on the tack room's wooden bench.

Everything Hank needed to use to repair anything, all the leather, sewing threads, awls, pins and screws, were in the properly marked boxes above the bench, just as his Uncle Clyde had arranged. All of his thoughts now drifted to his uncle and his legacy at the cow ranch.

After a very satisfying meal in the Palace Hotel dining room, Mary Anne and Cliff walked to the livery stable to pick up the sorrel team for their trip back home. Hiram McCoy greeted them with a smile and an arm load of squirming puppies.

"Which one ya want, folks? . . .Cliff, they were sired by your daddy's dog. And my dog, Molly, is their momma. They're all pure-breds. Pure as the snow in the 'Sierry-Petes'." Hiram was laughing and trying to hold the fidgeting puppies tight, as he spoke. "They's close 'nuf to bein' weaned, so you just as well take one along to home."

"Mighty nice! We'll give this little male pup to Hank and Abbey for their upcoming wedding anniversary," Cliff said.

"He looks exactly like Ranger," Mary Anne spoke, smiling, as she cradled a small bundle in her arms.

"Go ahead and load the wagon, honey, I may as well get this matter over with."

"You're going to the jail house to see your brother, aren't you, Cliff? That's what Abner Walsh told you last night at the supper table, right? Well, I'm going with you."

"Sure, you probably should, you're part of our family now, sweetheart," Clifton answered. "This most likely will turn into an ugly situation. I wish Hank would come riding around that building, yonder, but he has a score to settle with Getwood, so maybe it's just as well he isn't here. I guess I'd better see the sheriff first, though. C'mon, Mary Anne, we'll go over there together."

"I'm right sorry about all this, Cliff," Jim Sager spoke solemnly. "I'm very concerned for Lucille. She's been through so much, but having you and Mary Anne, and your baby boy at the ranch will sure help a lot."

* * *

Clifton slowly approached the cell and his "adopted brother" with a matter-of-fact appearance that divided his personality into separate thoughts. He remembered the occasions when they both worked very hard for Clyde, and how he and Hank and Getwood put in many a hard days work to build the fine herd the Circle Diamond carried.

He remembered the times when the family would be together, with his mother doting on Getwood as if to relieve some hidden guilt.

Now, as he came face-to-face with Getwood, Clifton suddenly became half-sick with disgust. How could this person damage the faith that some people held for him? How could he become so callous toward his mother? . . . and why would he steal? Was it for money? He had a good life for himself at the cow ranch. Why would he steal from his own ranch? And what about the despicable act he pulled on Abbey?

Clifton expected none of these questions to be answered, let alone answered truthfully, but he just had to ask Getwood all of these questions, anyway. He did remember what Hank said to him once. "He is not blood, Cliff, he's not worth doin' for."

Yet what probably disturbed Clifton the most was the effect this would all have on his mother. Could she truly survive the outcome of this debacle? The answer was a resounding yes!.

The only thing he could say to Get was, "I'm sorry for you, but you deserve everything that's coming to you - and I can't, and I won't - help you."

* * *

On their way back to the Circle Diamond, late that morning, Clifton and Mary Anne were very surprised to see a handsome bay horse being ridden across the ford at Caliénte Creek.

"S'matter," Clifton said, as he pulled rein on the sorrel team. "You havin' a go at runnin' the ranch by yourself, Cuz?"

"Oh, I got so caught up with all my work and chores, I thought I'd just mosey out for a "dude" ride, and enjoy this Nevada scenery of ours."

Hank winked at Mary Anne before he stepped down from the 'Lawyer', and bowed and swooped the ground widely, holding the stampede string tightly on his 'buckeroo' cowboy hat.

"I know you're a-lookin' for some more of those rustlers, Hank, and you can probably just turn your bay around and ride home with us. I'm pretty sure all the rustlins' stopped, at least for now," Cliff said. "With what I'm about to tell you, you can set your mind free of that mess. The big thing is, Hank, Getwood's in jail in Walker Lake, They got him dead to rights."

"Getwood . . . in jail? . . . in Walker? Who? How . . . well, tell me all about it." Hank was upset, but he was still questioning his cousin on the disposition of this miserable man with whom he was so very, thoroughly disgusted.

"The sheriff said they were waiting for the federal marshal to take him into Carson, where they said they'd incarcerate him, until his trial is set," Mary Anne said.

"Hank, there really isn't any reason for you to see him. They'll ask Abbey to sign some deposition of Getwood's actions at your cabin, and I will be a witness, too. Harry Carter will testify, and identify his cows the gang stole, and so can you and Cliff, at the appropriate time. Sheriff Sager said he' stop next week for a visit, and fill you in on everything."

"Well, thanks Mary Anne, for explaining this a little more. I still want to be certain nothing happens that could set Getwood free. I'm sure we can ease the pain that Aunt Lucy will have, especially with the presence of little Cody. Hey, w'-what the thunder is that a-wigglin' under your seat robe?"

"It was to be a surprise, but I don't see how anyone could hide a sweet, lil' puppy as this. Happy Anniversary to you and Abbey, I know she'll just love him," Mary Anne replied.

"Ought to, partner," said Cliff, smiling wildly. "It was Hiram's dog, Molly that whelped a litter of seven, and the daddy is ol' Ranger, Hiram said you'd get a pleasure out of havin' this little feller, here."

"I never said much about it , but I had a hard time gettin' over losin' Ranger to that badger. It came at a bad time, and I reckon this little guy will change my mind," Hank said as he playfully scratched the puppy's ears, before he mounted his favorite horse and headed home.

THE END

THE RUSTLER FROM CALIENTE CREEK

GLOSSARY

BARLOW.........cowboy pocket knife

BOSAL...........a part of the hackmore that fits over the horse's nose.

BRONCO.........or bronc; sometimes referred to as an onbroken horse. Wild.

CASTRATION....surgical rmoval of male horse's testicles. Renders them sterile.

CAVVY............sometimes spelled CAVY; a band of horses.

CHAPS............seatless leather over/pants used for protction; Spanish-Chaperos.

COULEE...........step ravine, especially in western U.S.A.

CUT...............(a) cattle separated from a herd and held together for some reason. (to) act of separating (cutting) cattle from a herd.

FARRIER..........horse shoer.

FOAL..............colt(m.) filly (f.) onder one year old.

GATHER...........when all the "cuts" and all the "jerks" have been made, it is that all stock is now a gather.

GELDING..........male castrated horse.

GREEN BROKE... horse with vert little training.

HACKAMORE.....bridle without a bit, of different designs.
Spanish- Jaquim(a).

HEADSTALL......part of bridle covering head,w/o bit.

...cont'.
HEIFER.......... a oung cow that has not borne young.

HORSE COLOR...(BASIC) bay, btown, sorrle & white.
(MAJOR) dun*, grey, palomino, pinto, (paint), roan, clay-bank* coyote*.

JERK.............when in rough country, only a small part is worked at a
time; one of these small drives is referred to as a jek.

JINGLE..........name given a corraled horse kept in camp or at ranch, to
use to bring in herd.

LASSO..........from Spanish la reata, meaning the rope.
A rope with a noose.

MALAPAI.......sometimes spelled MALAPI; kind of a slick, volcanic
rock.

MECATE........cotton rope attachd to bosal often looped around horse's
neck or open end at saddle.

MORRALL......canvas or leather bag with strap fitting over horse's head
in which to feed.

PINON.......any of several low growing pine trees in West

REATA........a catch rope of braided rawhide.

RODEAR......sometimes spelled RODEER; a round-up.

WIND-BROKE,,animal who'd once ben forced in long runs and injured
lungs.